To Frogard
I hope
me doesn't ~~~
after reading these. ☺
Enjoy!

The Vixen's Scream
Stories for the Worst in All of Us

By Fran Maglione

FRAN MAGLIONE

ISBN: 1517209463
ISBN-13: 978-1517209469

Cover design by Kevin Monahan

To Kevin, for always keeping me going, and to the two foxes that live behind our house, for their inability to keep tabs on each other.

CONTENTS

METAL

Jagged heavy metal music exploded out the door of the club and into the street. The sounds reverberated through the alleyways and over the sidewalks. A skinny boy with blue hair and a septum piercing walked into the club with three friends in tow. The boy scanned the room, nodding at acquaintances and smiling and waving at friends as he made his way through the crowd.

The music played on, growing louder as he walked farther into the club. The man on stage growled into the microphone as the guitars wailed behind him. The boy nodded his head to the beat, his concentration only interrupted by the feeling of something lightly bumping into his left shoulder.

He turned his head and was met with a fiery pair of hazel eyes and a smirk, topped with bright blond hair. The girl leaned in closely and spoke into his ear so he could hear her.

"Sorry, I get really into it sometimes. My name's Victoria," she said as she held out her hand.

"Trevor," the boy answered, shaking her hand. "Cool tattoo." He gestured to the red fox standing proudly on her upper arm, on display thanks to her sleeveless shirt.

"Thank you," she smiled. "I love them, so gorgeous and strong. You ever hear them call out to each other at night? It's called the Vixen's Scream. It sounds like a woman screaming bloody murder. It sounds pretty creepy if you don't know what you're hearing, but it's just the foxes trying to find each other."

"I've never heard one but that sounds pretty wild. I'll have to look it up when I get home," Trevor said with a smile.

She smiled warmly back at him and they both turned their attention to the stage once again, with Trevor internally praising himself for a successful conversation with a beautiful woman. He decided that he'd call that exchange a win and quit while he's ahead.

The singer screamed into the microphone as the bassist flailed around next to him on stage. A portion of the crowd was standing and watching, nodding their heads along with the music, while the rest was thrashing around in an overenthusiastic mosh pit in front of the stage. Arms and legs were flying all over the place as sweat and adrenaline filled the air.

Victoria started dancing around again, glancing back at Trevor with a shy smile every so often. She was met with an equally shy smile each time.

In a nearby corner of the club a pair of cold, dark eyes leered at Victoria. The menacing looking man with a silver lip ring appeared to be incredibly annoyed by Victoria's enthusiasm. He watched as she gleefully jumped around and started walking over to her, the booze inside of him deciding immediately that she was entirely too happy.

The man came up behind Victoria, hovering into her personal space, breathing heavily down the back of her neck. He pressed himself against her back and she pulled away in disgust, shooting him an angry glare.

When the man wrapped an arm around Victoria's waist Trevor took notice and stepped forward. Victoria slapped the man's arm away and stood next to Trevor, and both glared at the man while the music drowned out any chance of conversation.

The man strutted slowly over to Trevor, sweat and strong cologne flooding Trevor's senses. The man towered over him, and with one forceful shove he had Trevor on the floor. The man then grabbed Victoria's arm, but in an instant a group of men standing nearby surrounded him. Trevor's friends helped him up and tried to hold him back from angrily lunging at the man.

"Back off, we're trying to have a good time here," someone in the group said to the man, attempting to calmly ease his arm off of the girl.

Knowing he was outnumbered, the man put both hands up in a show of surrender as Victoria turned away in a huff and stomped out of the club. The placated mob turned back to the stage just as the guitar surged into a solo. With everyone distracted again, the man discreetly turned and followed Victoria's path out the door and down the sidewalk.

Immediately feeling herself being followed, Victoria quickly pulled out her cell phone. She started tapping a text message and hit "send" just as she turned a corner into an alleyway. She continued walking with purpose, fully sensing the man's presence behind her as she turned another corner.

Meanwhile, in different corners of the club, various cell phones began to beep and vibrate. Well-manicured hands picked up each phone to read the text, and then one by one each text receiver quickly marched out of the club.

Victoria picked up the pace, nervously looking around for some sort of reprieve. The man following her contorted his face into a sinister grin and chuckled softly at her fear.

The last person to get the text, mesmerized by the guitarist on stage, finally picked up her phone and read the message.

"Got one," it said. A smile spread across the girl's face as she headed out of the club.

Victoria felt strong hands grab her shoulders and spin her around, forcing her back against the wall of the alley. She stared into the steely eyes of the man, frightened by his predatory grin. The sudden clacking of multiple high heels entering the alley made the man pause and turn around in annoyance.

He was immediately faced with five women (or, at least,

what looked like women), staring at him with glowing red eyes. One of them was even licking her lips.

"What...what is this...?" the man sputtered.

Without a word the creatures descended on the man, changing their form as they attacked. Bearing fangs and sharp talons the demons tore into his flesh as he screamed in agony. Blood splattered around the alley and onto a nearby dumpster.

Victoria slowly walked over to the man, leaned over and buried her fangs into his neck, joining the feeding frenzy.

Inside the club, the music continued. Trevor sighed sadly as his friend leaned close and asked if he was ready to leave.

"Yeah, I'm ready. Sorry, but I don't really feel into this anymore," he answered with a frown.

The group of friends walked out of the club into the cool night air just as Victoria and her group appeared before them, back in human form, with the brunette in the back of the group viciously wiping her mouth clean with her sleeve.

"Hey there," Victoria purred with a smile.

"Oh, hey!" Trevor said, instantly back in a good mood. "I was wondering where you went. Are you okay?"

"Just fine," she smiled turning to gesture at her friends. "You guys want to go grab a bite to eat with us?"

"Sure!" Trevor answered as his friends nodded and smiled.

The groups walked together down the street toward the corner diner. In a nearby alley, blood pooled around a battered corpse that was picked clean, and a tarnished silver lip ring glittered in the moonlight next to a blood-splattered dumpster.

THE EXPERIMENT

The spinning wheel on the exercise bike joined the noises of the other equipment around Jessica: the treadmills, elliptical machines, stair-climbers, and weight machines. The panting and heavy breathing of everyone near her was drowned out by the symphony of machines, as well as the techno music blaring through her headphones.

She glanced at the digital clock on the bike, and when 30 minutes were up she slowed to a stop and chugged some water. A sudden feeling of being watched made her pause and look around. Seeing nothing suspicious, Jessica hopped off the bike and made her way to the locker room, smiling and waving at familiar faces as she went, even stopping to chat with a couple of them.

There was the married couple who always met there after work and lifted weights together, the treadmill guy who was a frightening clone of her ex but was much easier to talk to, and the trio of young men who seemed to watch themselves flex in the mirror more than they actually lifted weights.

Jessica pulled her dark hair back and smoothed the sides down as she twisted a hair tie around the ponytail. Beads of sweat still threatened to drip down her face as she picked up her gym bag and left the locker room. She glanced at her phone, flipping through text messages and the occasional rogue work email from an overachiever who was still working at 7:30 p.m. She rolled her eyes and stuck her phone back in her bag.

She said goodnight to the guy working at the front desk and pushed through the gym doors. As she walked out into the parking lot the breeze picked up, sending a chill up her sweaty spine. The uncomfortable feeling of being watched came back and stuck with her as she strolled to her car. She slowed down and looked around her, sighing and shaking her head when she, once again, saw nothing unusual.

"Chill, it's nothing," she told herself.

But, of course, it was something.

As soon as she started walking again she heard the dull thud of footsteps. Not high heels or even gym sneakers, but the thick clacking of a man's shoe; a loafer or maybe an oxford.

Before she could start listing off types of men's work boots in her mind, an arm reached around her and held a cloth over her nose and mouth. Jessica tried to scream, but the hand holding the cloth muffled her voice. The other arm wrapped itself tightly around her body as she struggled to free herself and to breathe. She suddenly felt very dizzy.

Everything started to go black, and Jessica slumped backward into the strong embrace of the stranger behind her.

*****

Jessica woke up on a cold cement floor. Her head was pounding and her wrists were hurting. She slowly opened her eyes, and as they focused she saw she was in a basement.

While trying to get up she realized that each of her wrists was wrapped tightly in a metal cuff that was attached to a chain. The two chains were joined together into one chain after several feet, and the whole system was secured to a hook that was drilled into the cement wall.

The reality of the situation flooded in like a tidal wave, and she suddenly felt terrified. She was alone in a basement and chained to a wall. Jessica started pulling at the chains, whimpering in fear, when she heard the clacking of a man's shoe again approaching the basement door.

The door opened slowly and a man descended the stairs. Jessica looked over at her abductor and took in his appearance: salt and pepper hair, slightly wrinkled and emotionless face, glasses, healthy physique, polo shirt, khakis, and loafers. It was loafers after all.

He was an appallingly average looking man, even handsome. He could have been an accountant, a teacher, an insurance salesman. Maybe he played golf on weekends, maybe he had children. For some reason, all of this made Jessica even more frightened.

The normal looking ones always seem to fool you. He was so quiet, so unassuming, people would say, he was the last person you'd think would do something horrible.

Yes, Jessica was certain that the normal looking ones were always the worst.

The man was holding a spiral notebook with a yellow cover and a black pen. As he reached the bottom of the stairs he stopped and stared at Jessica then began jotting something down in his notebook.

"What do you want with me?" Jessica asked with a shaky voice. "Why am I here?"

He looked up from his writing and stared at her blankly. He then resumed his writing.

Jessica decided to let him take the lead. Maybe she could win him over with kindness, go along with his plan to get ransom money, find out his intentions and offer him something he might want.

She shuddered at the thought of what he might want from her.

Finally, the man stopped writing and sat down on the bottom step. Jessica followed his lead and sat on the floor, trying to look as nonthreatening and obedient as possible. The man watched her then began writing again.

Jessica assumed that he was writing about her. She tried to assess the situation. What could he be writing? Was he observing her? Why?

He stopped writing again and the two of them simply stared at each other. After a few moments Jessica couldn't take it anymore and sighed loudly, trying hard to control her anger and fear.

"Well? Are you going to tell me anything?" she asked. "Can you at least tell me your name?"

"Henry," he muttered.

"Okay," Jessica responded, "now we're getting somewhere, Henry. My name is Jessica. Or did you already know that?"

"Interesting. And how did you deduce that I know you?" Henry asked as he started writing again.

"Well," Jessica hesitated, "you took me from the gym. I see a lot of people at the gym during the week when I go. Maybe you're one of them?"

"What would make you think that I'm a member of that gym?" he asked as he continued to write.

"Um…" Jessica thought, wary of his questions, "well, you seem to be in decent shape. Like, maybe you work out. And I remember in 'Silence of the Lambs' they said something about people coveting what they see every day. Wait, this isn't…like *that*, is it?"

Henry rolled his eyes as he wrote.

"I don't want your skin," he grumbled in annoyance.

"Okay, well, that's good," Jessica responded, though the answer only seemed to make her worry more. "So, what do you want?"

He continued writing without speaking while Jessica waited for an answer. Finally, he set down the notebook and pen and cleared his throat.

"You are an experiment."

Jessica's eyes grew wider and she inhaled sharply. She stayed quiet and waited for him to continue.

"I'm studying the human psyche and how it responds to isolation, torture and abuse. You seemed like a good subject. You are in good physical condition, you're young, and you appear to be very social, so I'd like to see how you react to being isolated," he said matter-of-factly.

Tears began to well in Jessica's eyes as her fear completely washed over her.

"When can I go home?" she whimpered.

Henry grabbed his notebook and stood up. He began walking back up the stairs without a word.

"Wait!" Jessica called. "Please, tell me, when is the experiment over?"

Henry paused at the top of the stairs, turned around and looked down at Jessica.

"When the subject is deceased," he said plainly.

He walked through the door and shut it, locking it behind him. Jessica began to sob softly.

*****

A couple of hours later the door opened and Henry walked down the stairs. Jessica was in the same position he left her in, sitting on the floor with a look of terror on her face. He opened his notebook and began writing again.

Jessica stared at him with wide eyes while he wrote. When he was finally finished he put his notebook down.

"Your chains are long enough to reach that bathroom over there," he said as he pointed to the right side of the basement. Jessica hadn't even noticed it before. It looked plain but well-equipped with a toilet, sink and shower stall. She suddenly wondered how many other people had been in her position and used that bathroom.

"Your personal hygiene is of the utmost importance," Henry continued with a slight shudder. He then sneered. "I will not come near you if you're not clean. You need to shower every day, and brush your teeth. There is a toothbrush and tube of toothpaste in there."

Jessica wondered if she would really be there long enough to use an entire tube of toothpaste.

"Since you just came from the gym, you should shower before you go to sleep. You're filthy," he said, cringing a little. "I have your gym bag with the clean clothes in it. I will bring it down so you don't put those sweaty things back on."

Great, Jessica thought, she'd been abducted by germaphobe.

"You have a mattress and a blanket to sleep on for now," Henry continued, gesturing to the makeshift bed in the left-hand corner. "I will provide your meals as I deem fit."

Certain that she wouldn't be winning any battles tonight Jessica decided to just obey the man until she could get her bearings. So, she simply nodded.

"Okay," she said, "whatever you say."

He began to write in his notebook again as Jessica sat quietly and watched him. When he was done he turned back to the stairs.

"Go shower now," he said with a grimace, "there's soap and towels in there." He then walked back up the stairs, shutting the door behind him.

Jessica took a deep breath and stood up.

"Guess I have to play the game," she said with a shaky voice then made her way to the bathroom.

Assessing what was around her, she took note of the hand soap, toothbrush and toothpaste that were left on the sink. There were rolls of toilet paper piled up in the corner, a lot of them, as well as stacks of disposable paper cups still in their packaging.

She opened the cabinet under the sink and found a litany of feminine hygiene products. And what appeared to be freshly laundered towels of varying sizes were hanging on several towel racks. She peeked into the shower stall and saw shampoo, conditioner, liquid soap, and a pink loofah hanging from the shower head – an actual loofah.

Jessica shook her head in disbelief, turned the water on and closed the bathroom door as much as her chains would allow. Showering in cuffs would be difficult. And didn't water rust metal? She looked at the cuffs and chain. They looked like stainless steel. Henry must have thought of that ahead of time.

Jessica then realized the predicament of removing her shirt, and then putting a new one back on, through the chains. She took another deep breath and walked out of the bathroom to stand at the bottom of the stairs, the chains only allowing her to just reach the bottom of the first step.

"Excuse me, Henry?" she yelled up the stairs. "I can't quite change my shirt through these chains. You don't want me to keep this sweaty one on, do you?"

After a moment she heard footsteps and the door opened. Henry walked downstairs, without his notebook, and looked uncomfortable.

"What...um...what size clothing are you?" he asked, avoiding eye contact.

"Uh...a small?" she answered.

He nodded and wandered back up the stairs and disappeared. Jessica stood there waiting, trying to listen to what he was doing. After a few moments she heard his footsteps return and his figure appeared at the top of the stairs holding a piece of blue fabric.

"You can put this on and rip that other shirt off," he said handing her a strapless cotton sundress. "You can put it on by stepping into it."

Jessica held the dress in her hands and shuddered. Who did this belong to, and where was she now? Jessica wasn't sure she really wanted to know.

"Okay," she said, faking a smile. "Thank you, Henry."

He turned around without a word and walked back up the stairs, closing the door behind him.

*****

After Jessica was showered and dressed she walked back out into the basement and started analyzing what was around her. Under the stairs were some dusty cardboard boxes and an old television. All of it was placed out of reach of the chains, though.

She walked over to where the chain was attached to the wall and examined it. She looked closely at the hook the chain was connected to. She felt it with her fingers and looked all around it and noticed something at the bottom of it: a tiny speck of what appeared to be rust.

"Well, it's a chance," she muttered with a small smile. She walked back into the bathroom and grabbed two paper cups. She filled one with water and walked back out to the hook. Holding the empty cup underneath to catch the runoff, she poured water all over the hook. Then she repeated the action.

"This may take a while," she said, "but at least now I've got something, you freak."

*****

It felt like she had only been asleep for a few hours when she heard the door open and sunlight poured down into the otherwise dim basement. She opened her eyes from her mattress and squinted up at Henry.

He descended the stairs holding a plate with a couple of waffles covered in some sort of jelly, and a glass of orange juice. His notebook was tucked under his arm. Without a word he bent over and placed the food and drink on the floor. He then stood back up and opened his notebook.

"Did you sleep?" he asked without looking at her.

"Um, yes, a little," Jessica answered.

He nodded and started writing.

"Well?" he asked.

"Well, what?"

"Did you sleep well?" he sighed in annoyance.

"Oh, uh, I guess?" she answered, trying to manage a small smile.

He scribbled more in his notebook then turned and walked back up the stairs and shut the door.

Jessica looked over at the food. Her stomach growled a little, realizing how long it had been since she last ate. She walked over to the food and crouched down to inspect it further. It looked normal enough. She picked up the plate and sniffed it. It smelled normal.

"Well, he plans to kill me anyway," she shrugged and picked up a waffle and took a bite.

She ate every crumb and drank every drop. Who knew

when she would be fed again? She then decided to earn a few extra points with Henry and immediately went to brush her teeth and shower again.

When she emerged from the shower she heard Henry coming down the stairs holding more fabric in one hand and his notebook in the other.

"All clean!" she said with a smile.

He looked at her blankly and handed her the dresses he was carrying.

"A few more so you're not wearing the same thing every day," he said. He then looked over at the empty plate and glass and nodded pensively. He opened his notebook and wrote briefly, and then he picked up the empty plate and glass and walked back upstairs.

Jessica sighed. Is this it? Is this the whole experiment?

No, it definitely wasn't.

*****

The next morning, Jessica awoke to a stinging pain on her face. She jerked upright on her mattress and tried to focus her eyes only to get the palm of a hand across her face.

"What the hell?!" she yelled out as she felt another slap. She covered her face and glared up at a kneeling Henry through the space between her arms.

Henry stared blankly at her as he sat back on his heels. He then picked up the notebook and wrote something down. In a fit of anger Jessica slapped the notebook away from him.

"What the hell was that about? Why did you hit me?!" she screamed at him.

Before she could blink a fist flew at her face, knocking her back onto the mattress. She lay there slightly disorientated for a moment as she heard Henry grab his notebook, stand up and walk back up the stairs.

After a few minutes Jessica got up and made her way to the bathroom. She looked in the mirror at her bruised face. She figured she would probably get a black eye from this. With a whimper she silently prayed that this would be the extent of

Henry's "torture" portion of the experiment, though somehow she knew it probably wouldn't be.

She took a deep breath and decided to start her day with a shower in hopes that she could ease tensions with Henry that way.

When she had climbed into the shower she heard Henry descending the stairs, then heard the telltale clatter of a dish and glass being placed on the cement floor before he immediately ascended the steps again. Jessica breathed a sigh of relief that he wasn't angry enough to starve her because of her actions.

After she finished cleaning up she walked over to the food. It looked like oatmeal but it had a strange odor to it. She thought maybe it was a new flavor she hadn't tried before. Not about to pass up a meal after she had clearly angered Henry, she started to eat. It didn't taste great, but she didn't really like oatmeal to begin with.

When she had finished off the bowl she walked back into the bathroom to grab her two paper cups, one filled with water, and walked back over to the hook on the wall to continue her rusting operation.

Suddenly her stomach lurched and she felt unbelievably queasy. Unable to control herself she dropped the cups and sped to the bathroom. She crouched over the toilet just in time to vomit an ungodly amount. She was certain it was the entire bowl of oatmeal. But her stomach wasn't finished yet. She kept retching, things she didn't even know were in her stomach flowed out. It burned her throat and made her eyes water, and her face hurt from the pressure of the vomiting adding to the pressure of the bruises.

As she continued to violently vomit she heard footsteps coming down the stairs. She started to sob as she couldn't make herself stop throwing up.

"What was in that oatmeal?!" she screamed over her shoulder before retching again.

Henry scribbled for a few moments in his notebook then paused and looked up at her.

"Ipecac," he said simply. "You're probably going to want to shower again." He then closed his notebook and walked back up the stairs.

"Son of a bitch," Jessica growled between retches.

When she was finally finished and felt like she could breathe again, she slowly stood up and splashed water on her face. She drank some water from the faucet then filled a paper cup.

Not only would she continue her rusting project, but she was going to focus all of her attention on it. She dipped her index finger and thumb in the cup and rubbed water all around the hook, focusing on the tiny speck of rust on the bottom.

When her fingers were wrinkled and she had used all of the water she put the cup down and got down on the floor. Slowly, she started doing pushups.

After several pushups she flipped onto her back and did some sit-ups. Jessica had decided that if this man was going to abuse her as part of his experiment, she was going to make sure she could at least put up a fight.

*****

After her workout she showered again, put on a fresh dress and resumed rubbing water on the hook.

What felt like several hours later, Henry came downstairs holding a plate of food again. It looked like simple white toast and a banana.

Not wanting to start a fight, Jessica stood up and folded her hands together in front of her. She flashed him a smile as he put the plate down.

"All clean again," she said brightly.

He nodded and opened his notebook, writing more. He then stood there watching her and waiting. It didn't take long before Jessica realized that he was waiting for her to eat the food.

Is this part of his experiment? She thought. Is that food poisoned, too? Or, is he trying to make her paranoid about all food? What is he trying to learn?

Jessica continued to hesitate and Henry resumed writing.

Finally, after a few moments Henry stared at her again.

The rumble of her empty stomach gave her away and she cautiously padded over to the food. She squatted down and picked up the banana. It was still in its peel, he couldn't possibly have done anything to it, she figured.

She gave it a quick smell, and getting only a normal banana odor she peeled it and took a bite as Henry nodded and jotted down more notes.

When she finished she put the peel down on the plate and stared at the toast. It did look inviting, but the butter that was spread on it was frightening her. He could have put something in it. The banana could have just been a decoy.

Henry was still staring at her blankly, so she picked up a piece of toast and pulled off part of the crust that was untouched by butter. She took a bite and Henry nodded again, taking more notes.

When she finished the crust she put the rest of the bread down and did the same thing with the other piece of bread. Then, she stepped back from the plate.

Henry grinned slightly as he wrote.

"Finished?" he asked smugly.

"Oh, yes," Jessica answered with a smile, "quite full. Thank you, Henry!"

He wrote once more then picked up the plate and walked back upstairs.

"Jackass," she muttered under her breath as he closed the door.

*****

The next morning, Jessica awoke to the sounds of the basement door being opened and a TV with its volume at the highest level blaring in another room upstairs. She rubbed her eyes and stretched, but froze when she heard someone say her name on the television.

She stood up and walked to the stairs, as far as her chains would go, and listened. It sounded like a morning news program.

"My name is Rose Franklin. I'm the mother of Jessica Franklin. Our daughter, Jessica, has been missing for three days and we have been told she was kidnapped from the parking lot of the local gym," a woman on the TV stated.

"Mom?" Jessica muttered as she strained to listen.

"I am addressing the man who has taken my daughter, Jessica," the voice continued. "Please, let Jessica go. She is an innocent young girl. She has never done anything cruel to anyone and tries to lead a good, wholesome, Christian life. Jessica is a good girl and we love her very much."

As Rose's voice cracked, Jessica could feel her eyes well with tears.

"Oh, mom," she sobbed. "I'm here. I can't get out but I'm alive."

"I know that you have a human heart, I know that you feel pain. I am pleading with you, the man who has taken my daughter, Jessica, please return her to me. You are bringing pain and suffering to her very loving family," Rose continued. "If you need help, if you are suffering, if you feel you are alone in the world, we can get you help. Just please don't make our daughter suffer because you are hurting. And Jessica, if you can hear me, we are trying to find you. We love you and we will find you."

"Mom!" Jessica screamed out, tears falling down her face. "I'm here, mom! I'm here! Oh, God, please find me."

Jessica fell to her knees and sobbed into her hands as she heard the TV turn off and Henry walk to the door. He stood at the top of the stairs watching her.

She lifted her head and stared up at him.

"Please," she pleaded, "let me go. My mom is hurting. I miss my mom so much. Please just let me go. I won't tell anyone who you are; I swear to God, I won't. Just let me go home."

She continued sobbing as Henry stared, a look that might have been pity briefly crossing his face. He sighed deeply and stared down at his shoes.

Jessica stopped crying and looked at him, hope slowly forming in her heart.

After a few moments it was shattered when he opened his notebook again and started writing.

"You heartless monster!" she screamed. "You don't care. You don't care at all. I'm a human being! You're destroying a human life for a stupid experiment."

She thrashed about in her chains and released a feral growl at Henry. After a few moments of watching her and writing, he turned around and closed the door.

"Son of a bitch!" Jessica screeched at the closed door.

*****

The following days and weeks turned into months, all bleeding together in a blur of anger, frustration, fear and sadness. Henry had begun alternating which meals were tainted and which weren't so Jessica would let her guard down only to be poisoned again. She began fearing the food he brought, no matter what it was.

One day he brought her a candy bar that was still in its wrapper. It was such a blessing that she hid it in the cabinet under the bathroom sink. She would turn to it when she was on the verge of starving to death as her one safe scrap of food.

Henry also alternated mornings when he would wake her with beatings. He had evolved from slaps to punches, even using his belt a few times to wake her with whips to her back or stomach. Jessica had stopped sleeping the entire night. She would wake after only a couple of hours and sit in the corner of the basement holding her knees against her chin and rocking back and forth, waiting for him.

When he would come downstairs and find her already awake he would scribble some notes down and go back upstairs.

One morning, Henry opened the door and walked down holding an MP3 player and some headphones. He placed them on the floor and walked back up the stairs. Jessica practically pounced on it, having not heard music in months.

She put on the headphones and started scrolling through the music, savoring every song as she reclined on her mattress, regardless of whether she had ever liked the singer before. She barely moved the entire day, just enjoying the music with a euphoric smile on her face.

The soft tones of jazz music put her to sleep that night. When she woke up to silence the next morning she saw that the battery had died overnight, as it was never fully charged to begin with. Jessica sobbed softly into the mattress for the next 20 minutes until Henry came down the stairs with breakfast.

Days later, she had even attempted to seduce him, hoping that would persuade him to be lenient on her. As he sat across from her one morning writing in his notebook, she placed a hand on his thigh, rubbing it softly, and smiled at him. The look of disgust and horror on his face would stay with her for a long time. He swatted her hand away and stood up, backing away so quickly he stumbled over his own feet before running back up the stairs. She didn't try that again.

Another time she came out of the shower to find her mattress missing. She had to attempt to sleep on the floor for three days until he finally gave her the mattress back. It took several more days for her back and neck to feel normal again, and for her body to be able to once again sleep for more than a few minutes at a time.

Through it all, Jessica continued her attempt to rust the hook that was keeping her attached to the wall. Every day, several times, she would bring a cup of water to the hook and rub and pour water all over it. The hook was visibly starting to rust all over, but not enough to break apart yet.

The routine of her daily life was slowly driving her insane. She would continue doing pushups and sit ups and lunges for as long as her meager energy allowed, but the lack of any other sort of stimulation was making her feel unbalanced. She even began to look forward to Henry coming downstairs because that meant she could talk to another human.

One afternoon, the basement door opened and Jessica sat up straight and stared up at him.

"What's the weather like outside?" she asked. "Is it Fall yet?"

He stayed silent as he placed a plate with a sandwich on it on the floor.

"Please talk to me. What's on the news lately? Am I still on the news? What did you have for dinner last night? Please just tell me something."

Henry pulled out his notebook and started writing.

Jessica felt her heart rate jump and she began breathing heavily, radiating anger.

"Writing, writing, writing," Jessica sneered. "You're always writing down your worthless thoughts in that stupid notebook. Would you like to know what this experiment is? Bullshit! It means nothing. You're just a sick freak. Of course keeping someone locked in a basement will mess with their head. You don't need an experiment to tell you that, you idiot!"

Henry paused and looked at her, slightly shocked by her words.

"Yeah, that's right. You're a moron and a freak!" she screamed, standing up quickly and stalking toward him. "And you're a coward. That might be the worst part. You can't even handle a small woman. You need to chain her up because you're scared of her. You're a wimp and a coward and a sick piece of garbage."

Henry dropped his hands to his sides and stared blankly at her.

"Oh, what's wrong, Dr. Psychopath? Don't want to jot any of that down? Don't want that for your records? That you're a pathetic waste of a life? I have a family and friends out there looking for me, missing me; people who love me. Who do you have, huh? Your victims? The girls who these dresses belonged to?" she said, gesturing to her clothes. "You're nothing. You're worthless. I might die in this basement, but I won't be alone. You will die alone, you pathetic coward."

After a moment Henry slowly crouched down and picked up the dish and started to turn back to the stairs.

"Hey, what are you doing? That's my food! You can't take

my food!" Jessica yelled after him.

She lunged forward and shoved him hard. He fell forward into the wall, dropping the plate on the stairs. He turned around, eyes burning with fury, and threw a punch across Jessica's face, knocking her onto the floor. He then stood over her and kicked her several times.

"The experiment is complete," he said through gritted teeth.

He then turned, stomped back up the stairs and slammed the door shut.

*****

It had been days since Henry had last been downstairs. Jessica knew it was over, that he wasn't going to come to the basement and feed her anymore. He was going to leave her there to die, and then bury her body somewhere no one would ever find it. She felt sadness for her family and friends who would never get closure and would never know what she went through.

She sat on her mattress and cried in her hands. She was so weak she could barely hold herself up to cry. Even breathing felt laborious.

After a few moments she slowly stood up and walked back over to the hook, plopping down next to it. She picked up the cup of water and resumed weakly rubbing water on the hook from where she sat on the floor, leaning against the wall as it held her up. She continued to sob silently until she even ran out of energy for that. Her arms fell to the floor and her head drooped forward, her chin resting on her chest. She could barely move, barely think. This must be what it feels like to die slowly, she thought.

A soft noise jerked her back into reality. She couldn't tell what the noise was at first. It sounded like a metallic pinging noise, like someone had dropped a penny on the floor or something like that. She turned to her right and saw that a piece of the hook had fallen onto the floor. It had rusted through.

Her eyes grew wide and she reached up trying to rub through the rest of the hook. It came apart in rusted pieces in her hand as her chain fell to the floor, no longer tethered to the wall.

Jessica was free.

But she wasn't out yet. She took a deep breath and assessed the situation. She needed enough energy to fight off Henry and get to a phone or get outside to a neighbor. She slowly stood up and walked to the bathroom and drank cup after cup of water. Then she reached into the cabinet under the sink and pulled out the candy bar, smiling softly.

"Thanks, Henry," she said with a grin as she ripped the wrapper open and took a huge bite.

She finished off the candy bar and continued guzzling water. After a few minutes she finally felt like she had some energy back. It was time to go home.

She needed to get Henry to come back to the basement, though. She knew he wouldn't respond to her yelling for him. Jessica would need to make a commotion that would prompt him to come back downstairs.

After looking around the basement for a moment, her eyes fell on a water pipe, the sound of water flowing through it as Henry used the kitchen sink upstairs. With a smirk she strolled over to it and wrapped her chain around a spot where two segments were connected.

She placed one foot on the wall for leverage and pulled as hard as she could with a loud grunt. Moments later the pipe ripped away from the wall with a loud clang, disconnecting from the rest of the system. Water burst out of the pipe and into the room.

Jessica smiled as she looked at her handiwork. Then, she heard the distinct sound of Henry rushing to the door.

The basement door burst open and Henry jogged down the stairs. He stopped at the bottom of the stairs and looked around, not seeing anything but the broken pipe and water pooled on the floor.

Behind him, a shadow crept closer to him. Before he could

react, Jessica wrapped her chain around his neck and pulled tight. Henry was on his knees in an instant, trying to grab the chain and gasp in some air.

Jessica did not let up and continued pulling the chains as hard as she could. When his struggling slowed she let go and roughly kicked the back of his head making him fall face-first onto the cement floor.

He lay there desperately trying to inhale through his damaged windpipe as Jessica walked over to the area underneath the stairs. She hoisted the old television into her arms and ambled over to Henry, who was still wheezing and holding onto his nose that was now gushing blood.

With rage in her eyes she released a piercing scream then lifted the television higher and slammed it down onto Henry's head.

He lay still on the floor under the TV as Jessica turned and walked up the stairs without so much as a glance behind her.

She walked through the doorway and shut the door, locking it behind her with the deadbolt that she was sure Henry had installed just for his experiments. She looked around, wary of someone else possibly being in the house, but saw no one. Ahead of her was the kitchen, so she slowly made her way to it. The house was immaculate, spotless, with a lingering smell of citrus-scented cleaning solution. She spotted a phone on the wall and dove toward it, immediately dialing 911.

"911, what is your emergency?" a woman's voice on the other line said. It felt so good to hear another voice that for a moment Jessica just sighed deeply and smiled.

"Hello?" the voice said again.

"Yes, hello, I need help. I'm being kept in someone's house. I've been here for a long time. I don't know where I am."

"Okay, try to stay calm, are you in immediate danger?"

"No, he's locked downstairs. I think he's unconscious," she said.

"We're tracing the call to where you are and we'll have police there in minutes, just hang tight," the woman said. "Can you tell me your name?"

"It's Jessica. Jessica Franklin."

There was a pause on the line.

"My goodness, many people have been looking for you for a long time, sweetheart," the woman said with a sad laugh. "I'm so happy to hear you're alive. Police will be there any minute now, honey, just hang on."

"Will you stay on the line with me while I wait for them?" Jessica asked with tears in her eyes. "You're the first human I've spoken to besides him in so long. I just...it feels good."

"Of course, Jessica, I won't go anywhere," the woman said. "My name is Marla, by the way. So, you said he was unconscious?"

"Yes, he's down in the basement. I threw a TV at him," Jessica answered.

Marla chuckled on the other line.

"Well, isn't that something," she said.

Suddenly, Jessica heard sirens.

"I hear them," she said, her breath catching and tears falling down her cheeks, "I hear the sirens, Marla. They're going to be here soon."

"You're going to be okay, sweetheart," Marla said. "Stand somewhere the police can see you when they come inside, okay? And keep your hands where they can see them. Just do what they tell you. They'll get you out of there and take care of you. Before you know it you'll be home safe."

Jessica heard the sound of police knocking the door down.

"Okay, they're coming in so I'm going to hang up now. Thank you, Marla," she said.

"You're welcome, Jessica. Good luck to you."

Jessica hung up the phone and sat on the floor in view of the front door with her back against the wall and her hands on her knees, a delirious grin on her face. She looked up at the kitchen table and noticed Henry's notebook sitting there. She was about to reach up to grab it but decided not to, sitting back down just as the police broke through the door. Jessica leaned her head back and closed her eyes as police yelled and ran around her.

After a few moments an officer knelt down beside her. She turned and smiled wide at him.

"Hi there," she said.

"Hello. Is there anyone else in the house that you know of?" he asked.

"Just Henry," she said, pointing to the basement door. "He might still be unconscious though."

Several of the officers paused and exchanged looks of disbelief as two more opened the basement door and stalked down the stairs, guns drawn.

The officers reached the bottom of the stairs and stared at the bloody mess on the floor in front of them.

"Damn," one of them said with a chuckle. "She wasn't kidding."

Upstairs the officer helped Jessica stand up, her chains dangling and bumping into the wall, and walked her toward the front door.

"Don't worry, we'll get these off of you and get you some medical attention," he said. "Are you hurt badly? You look a little bruised."

"He beat me," she said, "and he starved me. But that's it."

"Oh, is that it?" he chuckled.

As Jessica stepped outside, the bright light of the sun blinded her for a moment. She held her hand over her eyes to block the powerful glare that she hadn't seen in months. When she started to adjust to the sun she slowly made her way to the police car, the officer following behind her.

She knew she'd be spending the rest of the day at the police station answering question after question and giving statements while people stood around her taking notes.

She also knew she had no plans to shower that day.

ROGERS ISLAND

Olivia tiptoed gracefully over slick rocks and shells, her rubber boots struggling to catch a grip on the smooth surfaces as they walked farther away from the shore and into the cold wind of the sandbar. Elijah confidently stomped forward ahead of her, intent on stepping in every small pool of water he could find.

"Slow down!" she called out to him. "I don't know how you're keeping your balance. I can barely walk on these damn rocks."

"We don't have that long before the tide comes back in," he called over his shoulder. "We need to keep moving or we'll be stranded out there. This land bridge is only uncovered for like a half hour and there's no one around to even know we're out there."

Olivia rolled her eyes and stumbled forward, trying to keep up without falling into the water of the bay that splashed onto the thin sandbar from both sides. Rogers Island was getting closer, the imposing tide island sitting alone half a mile from the shore clustered with half-dead trees and the remnants of a building. They were alone – the hidden beach littered with "No Trespassing" signs and surrounded by a fence that they had cut their way through with wire cutters.

"What used to be here?" Olivia asked, eyeing the chunks of

brick foundation and broken pieces of walls she spotted through the sparse trees.

"You'll see," Elijah answered with a grin. He'd been researching the history of the island for weeks before he finally snapped and decided to take a road trip out there. Referred to as The Cursed Island by locals, people tended to stay away from the area entirely. There were a lot of myths about that place, all of them intriguing to Elijah. From the story of pirates burying cursed treasure in its sand, to the tale of a witch who haunted the trees and made them come to life, Elijah wanted to hear it all.

Once the pair stepped onto the island, Elijah led them closer to one of the old buildings that still stood intact. He stepped up to a large bush and pushed it away revealing a worn down sign that read: Carl Rogers Psychiatric Asylum.

Olivia raised an eyebrow.

"A mental hospital?" she asked.

"Well, sort of. In the 1940s and 50s they used to send people out here that were considered dangerous. They called them crazy, but I don't believe any of them actually were. People wanted to get rid of them. I think they were just different – maybe had scary thoughts and ideas or just acted differently, and there was no legal reason to lock them in jail. But the treatments they received here were pretty messed up. It was a really controversial place."

Elijah stared pensively at the building for a moment then started walking toward it.

"Wait, we're not going in there, are we?" Olivia cringed.

"Of course we are! Why do you think we came out here?" he answered. "I just want to check it out. It'll take a minute. Come on, it'll be really cool, I promise."

After a long pause and a deep sigh, Olivia stepped forward and followed Elijah. The pair walked through the underbrush and skeletal, dying trees. The asylum's main building loomed before them.

"How in the world is that building still standing in good condition?" Olivia asked.

"I read that the other buildings around it protected it from flooding and stuff. I guess it hasn't been exposed as much as the others," he answered. "Or maybe it's the curse."

Olivia rolled her eyes. As they walked up to the door, the sound of buzzing came into earshot and grew louder as they got closer. Elijah looked down and saw a swarm of flies buzzing around the rotting remains of several rats and possums.

"Whoa. What do you think did that?!" he exclaimed, gesturing to the mess.

"Oh, gross!" Olivia yelled as she started backing away.

"Come on, it was probably a coyote or something that got trapped out here when the tide came in."

Olivia stood still, continuing to stare at the remains. Elijah stepped toward her and placed a hand on her arm.

"It's okay, it's probably nothing. Maybe these animals just ran out of food and died of starvation. Who knows?" he said.

The two side-stepped the corpses and walked up to the door. The hinges were rusted, the door barely holding on. Elijah lightly pushed the door and it fell to the ground with a loud slam.

"Yeah, we're being really discreet here, aren't we?" Olivia said as she stepped through the entrance. "Let's just go look at your precious creepy hospital before the locals hear all the noise out here and send cops after us."

Elijah hesitated then quickly turned around and looked behind him.

"What, Mr. Adventure? What's the problem?" Olivia asked.

"Nothing, I just...I thought I heard something," he answered.

As they continued inside Elijah pulled out his cell phone and turned on the flashlight function so he could guide the way. Chairs and sofas in various states of decomposition littered the room, and a large half-circle desk sat in the middle with old, tattered papers still scattered all over it. Garbage, sand, shells and rocks were strewn about the floor.

"So, what was this, the reception area or something?"

Olivia asked.

"Yeah, I think this is where guests would sign in to visit the patients," he answered.

A heavy thud on the carpet behind them made them both jump and spin around to look. Elijah shined the flashlight on the corner the sound came from. A large ledger was on the ground with the words "Guest Book" printed on it in script. Elijah walked over and picked it up.

"Oh, man, look at this! It's got signatures of people who visited here. Check out this one: June 13, 1947."

As Elijah flipped through the book, Olivia walked closer and looked over his shoulder at all of the names scribbled on the pages.

"That one shows up a lot," she said, pointing to a recurring name in the ledger.

"Thomas Brown," Elijah read. "Well, I guess he had a relative here."

"Maybe, but wow, he came here multiple times every single day. That's devotion," she said.

Elijah continued flipping through the pages and watching the years increase until they both noticed something that made their stomachs drop.

"Wait a minute," Elijah said as he kept turning pages. "1962? But this place closed down in 1959."

The years continued on, with only one name written in the ledger: Thomas Brown.

"Why did he keep coming here and writing his name?" Olivia asked. "Or did he? Did someone just come here and do this as a prank maybe?"

"It's the same handwriting throughout, even the early years," Elijah answered. "Wait, look..."

As he flipped to the back of the ledger the years entered the 2000s.

"How is he still alive and able to come here?" Olivia asked, her voice beginning to shake.

They finally flipped to the last page in the ledger and read the day's date: March 14, 2015.

"Oh, my God," Elijah gasped as he dropped the book. "That's today's date."

"We need to leave now," Olivia answered as she looked around. "Someone is severely messing with us. Yes, it's just someone messing with us. We know you're here! Just come out! It's not funny!"

They heard nothing. Finally, Olivia released an exasperated sigh and turned and walked toward the door.

"I'm gone. This place can shove it," she said. But just as she walked to the entrance expecting to walk over the fallen door, she saw that it had been returned to its hinges and was now closed.

"What the hell is going on? Who is doing this?" she yelled as she turned to Elijah. He was frozen in fear staring at the door. As he approached it and grabbed the knob, he found it was locked from the outside and wouldn't budge.

"That's not possible," he said as he started slamming his body into the door. "This isn't possible! Why won't it open?"

Olivia grabbed his arm and pulled him in the opposite direction.

"There has to be another exit," she said. "Come on. Someone is definitely messing with us and I will not be someone's sucker."

Olivia pulled Elijah down the hallway, farther into the building. She grabbed his cell phone out of his hand and pointed it ahead of them until she spotted another door with light peeking through its cracks at the end of the hallway.

"There we go, an exit," she said as the two jogged down the corridor. Elijah didn't hesitate to slam himself against the door, and when it burst open and fell onto the ground Olivia breathed a sigh of relief.

"See? Dumb punk forgot to lock this one," she said as she turned around. "We're on to you, dumbass!"

They walked outside and looked around. They were deeper into the island now, and tall reeds surrounded them swaying in the breeze.

"So, which way do we go?" Olivia asked, trying to hide the

panic in her voice.

"Let's just try to get to the water then we can follow it around back to the land bridge," Elijah answered.

The two plowed forward into the reeds, trying to part them and push through. They stumbled and tripped over the tall plants trying to walk in a straight line to the shore. After what seemed like a few minutes too long, Elijah pushed through the last row of plants and hopped out into the open expecting to be greeted with waves lapping against rocks. Instead they were greeted with the sight of the building they had just left.

"That's impossible," Elijah muttered. "We were walking away from it."

Olivia swallowed loudly then took a deep breath.

"I think there's more to that curse story than we think," she said, staring gravely at the building in front of her.

Elijah turned to the right and started walking around the outside of the building and toward the front door they had initially entered. Olivia followed behind, and as they reached the door and turned to find the path they had entered on when they first stepped onto the island, they found it overgrown and covered with more reeds and grass.

"Should we even try getting through all of that?" Olivia sighed.

Elijah started breathing heavy, and with a loud growl he jumped forward and threw himself into the reeds as he heard Olivia calling after him. He landed in the sand with a thud, spitting some out of his mouth, and stood up. He was back on the beach, but the land bridge was nowhere to be seen. In its place were continuous raging waves of ocean water that slammed against the island. He heard Olivia walk up behind him.

"So I guess the tide clock has no meaning here on Freak Island," she said in annoyance. "This is ridiculous. Let's just swim back – it's only half a mile."

"We'll freeze!" Elijah yelled. "And look at that rip tide, it'll pull us under."

The moment Elijah mentioned the rip tide the water picked

up speed and became more violent.

"We're not going anywhere," he said grimly.

Olivia took a deep breath and tried to think.

"Then we need to find out more about what we're dealing with," she said. "Come on, we need to go back inside."

She turned and pushed forward once again toward the building. After briefly hesitating, Elijah sighed and followed.

Olivia pushed open the door to the main building, which once again fell off its hinges and onto the floor. She stepped over it and walked to the desk and started looking around for something that would help. Elijah slowly joined her, holding his glowing phone up and staring wide-eyed around the room.

"Wait a minute," he said as he looked at his hand, "my phone!"

Olivia rolled her eyes again.

"Bet you 10 bucks it has no service," she said.

Elijah looked and groaned angrily at the "NO SERVICE" text displayed on the top left corner of the screen.

"Just calm down," she said. "Something wants us here, wants to keep us here, and I think there's a reason. I've seen enough horror movies to know that something bad happened here and someone needs some avenging or whatever."

"What about that guy we saw in the book?" he said. "The guy who kept signing in every day. Thomas."

"Yes! That's right. Let's see," Olivia said as she flipped through the front desk's paperwork. "Well, here's a map of the grounds. Maybe if we walk over to the residential halls we can find the room the guy was visiting. What does it say in the ledger? What room did he visit?"

Elijah walked over to the book on the floor and picked it up.

"Room 207," he said. "Every day, room 207."

"Well, let's go find room 207," Olivia shrugged.

"How in the hell are you so calm right now?" Elijah asked. "You lose your mind when you see an ant crawling on your shoe."

"Honestly? I don't know," she answered. "I just don't think

that whatever it is wants to hurt us. I mean, it would have hurt us already. I think it just wants our help."

After exchanging a quick look of disbelief and a shrug, they turned and made their way out the back door toward the remnants of the other building. Elijah turned his phone's flashlight on again as they made their way inside and through the halls. They saw that the room numbers were only in the 100s.

"I guess we'll need to go to the second floor," Olivia said with a grimace, looking over at the dark, imposing staircase. "The creepiness factor here is on point, that's for sure."

"We came this far. Can't stop now," Elijah answered as he made his way forward.

The two clutched each other as they slowly crept up the staircase to the door of the second floor. Elijah pushed it open and held his phone in front of him. The hallway was still and empty aside from papers scattered about and a couple of overturned filing cabinets. He stared at the numbers on each door.

"The odd numbers are on this side," he said, pointing to their left. They crept forward until they reached 207. After a pause, Elijah pushed open the door.

The room was bare aside from a bed and an armchair. In the corner they spotted a small old man with his back to the door wearing a brown suit, looking out the window and lightly sobbing. Elijah froze and silently looked over at Olivia. Olivia straightened her shoulders and stepped forward into the room.

"Thomas? Thomas Brown?" she asked in a gentle voice.

The man turned to face them displaying sad, bloodshot eyes and disheveled, thinning hair. His frown slowly turned into a little smile.

"You found me. I can't believe someone finally found me. I can go home now," he said with relief. Tears started forming in his eyes. "I can be free."

Olivia smiled.

"We want to help you. Tell us what we can do," she said.

"Why are you trapped here?" Elijah asked.

"My wife was a patient here many years ago. Her name was Beatrice. They sent her here because they said she was dangerous. They didn't know the real story. Nobody knew, but she was a witch. She was an evil spirit and she kept my soul locked in this room with her, only to be freed by kind souls like yours," he said with a smile.

"Wow," Elijah breathed with a grin, looking over at Olivia. "That's amazing. There actually was a witch."

Olivia looked back at Thomas in awe.

"Is all of that really true?" she asked.

Thomas paused and turned back to the window. Slowly he started to chuckle.

"No," he said as he turned back to face them. Suddenly, his slow, dark and sinister laugh was joined by a woman's cackle. Olivia and Elijah started backing away in fear only to hear the door behind them slam shut.

On the opposite wall, a dark shadow formed. It slowly took shape into a wrinkled and skeletal old woman's body draped with a tattered black shroud. The woman floated over to the couple, her feet dangling from her bony legs. Thomas slowly ambled over to her side.

"Who are you? What do you want from us?" yelled Olivia.

"My dear Thomas, my sweet Thomas," the old woman said as she turned to him, "such a good husband, in life and in death. You're always bringing me presents."

Olivia and Elijah turned and tried to beat the door down while twisting the knob in vain to get away.

"It's been so long since I've had fresh meat; really good meat, too. I'm so tired of rats," she said with disgust as she slowly floated toward them.

"If you wanted to eat us why didn't you just do it instead of making us go through all this crap?" Elijah yelled.

"Darling," she said with a smirk as she crept closer to him, "I'm bound to this building now. The curse keeps me here forever, but luckily I have my Thomas to help me. He keeps me fed and happy."

"Happy wife, happy life," Thomas said with a grin.

"Furthermore, do you know how simply boring it is being trapped on an island for all eternity?" she added.

With a final cackle, the old woman flew onto Elijah. Her teeth ripped through his flesh as his scream mixed with Olivia's, echoing through the corridors of the empty hospital.

THE HOUSE

"Alex, look at this place! It's beautiful!" Emmy exclaimed from the entrance, a huge grin on her face as she looked around.

"Yeah, it's fine so far. Let's actually walk inside first," her husband answered with a smirk.

Emmy glared at Alex and walked farther inside the entryway, the real estate agent close behind.

"And you'll see the kitchen has brand new stainless steel appliances, a really great value," the agent said in her best salesperson voice.

Alex walked into the kitchen and examined the stove. He asked the agent if the neighborhood had gas lines, or if there were any future plans for gas lines, as Emmy continued to wander around in awe of the house.

She slowly strolled through a hallway into the den, running her hand along the wall. It felt warm to her, which was strange. It felt comforting, though, and safe.

She stood in the hallway and placed both palms flat against the wall and closed her eyes. Breathing deeply she smiled and felt a sort of connection with the house.

Suddenly her eyes flew open with a start and she pulled her hands away. She could have sworn the wall had vibrated slightly. After a moment she turned and headed back toward the others.

"I like the island in the middle of the kitchen, and there are plenty of outlets," Alex said as Emmy walked in. "We're going to need to do something about this ugly paint job, though."

"Right, right," she said in a daze.

"Are you okay? You look like you just saw a ghost," Alex said as he turned to the agent and chuckled. "Is this place haunted or something?"

"Oh, no, no one has died here," the agent answered. "It's not haunted, that's for sure."

"Stop it, Alex, it was nothing," Emmy said, rolling her eyes. "Don't creep people out. I like this place. I like it a lot. It feels nice."

"It feels nice?" Alex said with a smirk. "Right, great, the house feels nice."

He chuckled and walked into the dining room, the agent hot on his heels. They discussed the chandelier that the previous owner had left behind as part of the sale.

Emmy felt a strong feeling of warmth flowing through her. There was something about this house. It felt cozy, loving and familiar. This was meant to be her home, she just knew it.

When they all made it down to the basement, Alex noticed something unusual.

"Is that a door that's been painted over?" he asked.

"Yes, apparently that was an old wine cellar that hasn't been used in years," the agent said. "It's very moldy and musty in there so one of the previous owners just sealed the door shut and painted over it. You can always put up a wall panel or a shelving unit in front of it if you think it's ugly."

As the trio walked through the rest of the house, Emmy kept running her hands along the walls as she walked. Making physical contact with the house felt comforting to her. Despite Alex warning her several times about scuffing up the paint job, she didn't stop.

When they had walked through the entire house they stood outside on the front porch with the agent. She and Alex discussed the possibility of making an offer and what they would need to do to make that happen. Emmy smiled.

"We're definitely going to make an offer," she said to no one in particular.

The agent and Alex paused.

"Uh, honey, maybe we should talk about it before making statements like that," Alex said.

"There's nothing to talk about," Emmy replied plainly. "This place is my home."

Alex and the agent exchanged confused glances.

"Well, give me a call if and when you're ready to make a real offer," the agent said. "This place won't be available for long, I'm sure. It's a foreclosure so this price is rock-bottom. Take care!"

The agent walked quickly to her car, leaving Alex to stare confused at Emmy.

"You're acting weird," he said. "You're, like, obsessed with this house."

"I'm not obsessed," she replied. "I just feel like this is our home, that's all."

"Yeah, great, let's go to our actual home now, okay?" Alex reached out and took her arm, guiding her back to their car.

That night Emmy tossed and turned in their bed. With a sigh she rolled onto her back and stared at the ceiling of their cramped apartment. She couldn't stop thinking about the house. She thought about how she'd decorate it, how their furniture would fit, what the house would look like in different seasons throughout the year, and what sides of the house the sun would rise and set on. All she could think about was the house.

Her last thoughts before finally drifting off to sleep were of the warm feeling she got when she held her hand against the walls.

*****

The next morning, Emmy woke to find Alex no longer in the bed. She got up and found him in the living room sitting on the couch with his laptop.

"Morning," Emmy said sleepily. "What are you looking at so early?"

"I wanted to know more about that house," Alex said. "You know, if we're serious about an offer."

Emmy smiled wide and hopped onto the couch next to him. She wrapped her arms around his neck and kissed his face over and over.

"All right, all right," he said with a laugh. "Don't get too excited yet. This house is kind of weird."

Alex showed Emmy the listing he was looking at.

"It says here it's had quite a few different owners in the short time since it was built, and each time the house would go into foreclosure," he said.

"So? Maybe the house has a big problem no one could afford to deal with. We'll get a home inspection and find out," Emmy replied.

"Well, I'd like to ask our agent a few more questions first. I just want to make sure we're not making a huge mistake here," he said.

Seeing Emmy's excitement wane, he leaned in and kissed her forehead.

"I just want to get us the best house I possibly can," he whispered. "I want us to be happy and safe in a good home, that's all. We'll get the full story, don't worry. I'm sure it'll be fine. Before you know it we'll be painting walls."

Emmy smiled again and leaned in for a kiss.

"This calls for pancakes," she said, leaping up from the couch and jogging into the kitchen.

*****

Several hours later the two found themselves sitting in their real estate agent's office, a large batch of papers spread out in front of them listing previous owners and how much the house sold for. It was first built in 1987 for a young couple. Five years later it was foreclosed and a middle-aged couple bought it. Ten years after that a single young man bought it. Just three years later, it went to a couple and their daughter, and five years after that a family of four bought it. Then it went to Emmy and Alex.

"So, basically everyone who bought this house defaulted on it, and the bank sold it to the next owner. No contact was ever made between the buyers and any previous owners," Alex said.

"Well, yes, but that's pretty standard in a foreclosure," the agent replied. "It becomes the bank's property so they handle the sale."

"Why did everyone default on it?" he asked.

"There are many reasons why that happens," the agent answered, "loss of a job or primary income, falling behind on payments, a divorce or a couple splits up and one person can't afford the house on their own. I don't really know, Alex. To be honest, it's not our business to know that sort of thing."

"It just seems weird, doesn't it? Suspicious?" he prodded.

"It is unusual, yes, but that's it," she said, "just a rare occurrence. Not out of the realm of possibility to happen, just rare. Now, would you like to make an offer? I have a few other people that might be interested in seeing this house."

"Yes!" Emmy yelled as she stood up. "We want to make an offer. Tell them they can't see it."

Alex turned and looked at her, eyes wide. She looked back at him, confident and assured, nodding and smiling.

"Well, uh, I guess we're making an offer," he shrugged.

*****

A few weeks later the couple was stumbling into the house carrying heavy boxes that came from a gradually emptying moving truck.

"Aren't you supposed to carry me over the threshold?" Emmy asked with a smirk.

"I'm carrying these boxes over. That'll do for now," he answered.

Emmy groaned loudly as Alex sighed and put down the boxes he was holding. He playfully pushed her back out the door then picked her up, carrying her into the house bridal style.

"That's better," Emmy said, kissing his cheek before hopping back down to the floor.

Emmy wandered around the house touching the walls and feeling complete tranquility.

"I'm so glad we got this house," she said.

"I know, you've said that about 57 times now," Alex chuckled.

"Well, it's true."

Alex walked around the living room contemplating future jobs they'd need to do.

"We'll have to get the chimney swept before we use the fireplace. And we'll have to get the furnace serviced. Hopefully we can get someone in soon to give us a quote on redoing the kitchen cabinets and countertops," he said.

Emmy froze in place and cringed picturing how many strangers would be wandering through her home in the coming weeks.

"What's wrong?" Alex asked. "You knew we'd have a few things to do when we moved in."

"Nothing, I just..." Emmy started. "I don't like the idea of so many random people roaming around my home."

Alex stared confused at Emmy, opening his mouth to talk but shutting it immediately. He shrugged and sighed then walked away.

Even Emmy was surprised at herself. Why did she care if some contractors came into the house? She hadn't even been living there a week yet. Although, everything seemed to feel weird and confusing to her lately, except for the house. The house always felt comforting and right.

*****

Days later, Emmy was home from work waiting anxiously for the house guests. Alex had scheduled a furnace technician, chimney sweep and electrician all on the same day. By some horrific coincidence they all arrived around the same time. The doorbell kept ringing as Emmy tried to keep herself calm.

The men worked downstairs while Emmy hid upstairs in the master closet. She sat on the floor trying to calm herself down. She heard them all talking to each other downstairs, and the noise made her feel more on edge. Her breathing sped up and she was unable to relax. She started whimpering in the closet and hugging her knees as she tried to focus on the house around her.

"Why won't they leave?" she asked herself. "They've been here for hours. Just leave already."

Suddenly, the house started to vibrate around her. She focused her attention and it began to shake violently. She heard the men downstairs panicking and yelling before she finally heard multiple footsteps running out of the house.

Emmy sat in the closet and smiled. The house was hers again.

*****

Hours later Alex returned home, walking around the house and surveying the work. He stopped midway through and called out to Emmy.

She came strolling downstairs with a smile.

"What's up?" she asked innocently.

"It looks like none of them finished their work," he said. "What happened here?"

"I didn't want them here," she answered, "so I made them leave."

"You what? What exactly did you do?"

"Nothing, it was the house."

Alex stared blankly at her for a few moments. He was completely without words. Finally, he shook his head and walked away, but Emmy was close behind him.

"Don't ignore me, Alex. I'm not lying to you. It was the house," she insisted.

"I don't care about your weird fantasies or your imagination. I want to know why the hell these guys I paid didn't finish working on my house," he answered.

"Your house? This is my house, too, remember," she said,

growing irritated.

"Yeah, I get it. You're obsessed with the house. Cool it," Alex said.

Suddenly, Alex felt the house start to shake.

"What the hell...?" he said, looking around.

"Oh, I should cool it? Should I really cool it, Alex?" Emmy said as she walked slowly toward him.

"What is the matter with you?" he yelled. "Why are you acting so crazy? Chill out. It's me, remember?"

The house began shaking violently again, and dishes were beginning to fall from the cabinets.

"Stop this freaking house from shaking!" Alex screamed in desperation.

And, as if someone had flipped a switch, the house stopped.

Alex looked at Emmy in horror. She stared calmly right back at him.

"There is more to this house than you know," she said.

"Yeah, no kidding," he answered.

*****

After hearing the three contractors recall the events of their day in the shaking house, Alex spent most of the next few days avoiding Emmy, and trying to stay out of the house as much as possible when he wasn't at work.

He was out in the front yard mindlessly pulling weeds while Emmy sat on the floor in the middle of the upstairs closet again. She breathed deeply with her eyes closed trying to somehow reconnect with the house and calm herself down. She couldn't hear the house, sense it, or feel any control over it, all she knew was that simply being in the house and making physical contact with it was enough to make her feel safe.

She wished she had more power over it, though. Was it her anger that controlled it, her fear? The house seemed to know what she was thinking, but not the other way around.

Alex came back inside and called out to Emmy. He walked upstairs and saw the light in the closet on. He sighed and shook his head as he walked over and opened the closet door to find her sitting cross-legged on the floor.

"Look, I don't even want to know why you're in here. I just wanted to tell you that I'm going to go stay with my brother for a few days," he said. "I don't know what's going on here, but I really don't like it. You've changed and you're kind of scaring me now."

Tears started to well up in Emmy's eyes.

"You don't have to be scared," she said, jumping to her feet and reaching out to him. "Really, you don't. It won't hurt you, I would never hurt you!"

"Emmy, listen to yourself," he replied. "You sound crazy. This house is dangerous. I don't know if it's on a fault line or what, but I don't feel safe in here anymore."

"You're safe, we're both safe. It'll keep us safe," Emmy said, gripping her hands tightly to the front of his shirt.

Alex slowly put his hands on Emmy's and carefully lifted them off his shirt.

"I'll be back in a few days," he said, and then walked out of the room leaving Emmy standing helpless in the closet with tears in her eyes.

*****

It had been three days since Alex left. Emmy had called his phone and sent him text messages begging him to come back, saying she would stop talking about the house and everything would go back to normal. Alex ignored all of her pleas, simply sending one text message that repeated what he had said before he left: "I'll be back in a few days."

Whether that meant for good or simply to pick up his stuff and leave again remained to be seen.

Emmy sat alone on the couch, trying to read a book but unable to get beyond the first few sentences. She felt miserable, and for once the house wasn't making her feel better.

In fact, the house had fallen silent, not really showing its presence anymore, and for some reason this made Emmy feel uneasy.

She went to the cabinet in the kitchen and pulled out a bottle of wine. If she was going to be miserable she was at least going to be drunk and miserable. As she went to grab a glass she heard a noise outside. It sounded like someone walking through leaves, and then walking on the deck. Then she heard hushed voices.

"You sure they ain't home?" one of the voices asked.

"I told you, they left days ago. Haven't seen them come back," a second voice answered.

Emmy started to panic. She didn't want these strange men coming in and finding her here alone. Who knows what they would do to her?

She ran over to the knife holder on the counter and pulled out the largest knife. Breathing erratically she stood in the kitchen, holding it with both hands while waiting and listening. She heard something cutting through the glass on the sliding glass door to the deck.

Emmy wasn't exactly sure what she'd do once they came inside. Wave the knife around? Scream loudly to disorient them? She hoped they didn't have a gun. Suddenly she realized that she should have called 911, but her phone was charging upstairs.

She really hoped they didn't have a gun.

"No," she whimpered. "Don't let them come in."

Suddenly the house started to shake lightly.

"What was that?" one of the men asked.

"What was what?" the other answered.

They finished cutting a hole the glass and Emmy saw a gloved hand reach in and unlock the sliding door. They slid it open and the house started shaking violently, and then stopped.

"Whoa, was that an earthquake?" one of them asked.

"Oh, crap! Jimmy, look, there's someone here!" the other said, pointing at Emmy.

Emmy held the knife up, a wild look in her eyes.

"Don't come any closer!" she screamed. "Stay away! Get out of my house!"

"Easy there, sweetheart, don't do anything stupid," Jimmy said as he approached her, grinning.

Emmy backed up into a wall and started panicking just as the house began to shake again.

"What is going on in this house?" the other man asked.

Suddenly, books started falling off the bookshelf in the living room. Then the knife holder in the kitchen shifted forward on the counter and moved closer to the edge. It fell with a loud bang and the knives spread all over the floor. One of them seemed to stand up on its own.

"What the hell is doing that?" the other man asked, panic rising in his voice.

The knife then quickly shot through the air impaling itself in the left shoulder of Jimmy. He screamed in pain as another knife flew through the air and sliced open his neck. He fell to the floor twitching and choking, blood pouring from his wounds. A final knife through his chest silenced him. Emmy watched with a blank expression.

The other man screamed. He turned to run out of the house only to be stopped by the glass door quickly sliding shut in front of him.

Emmy slowly walked toward him.

"You should not have come here," she said, as he desperately clawed at the door trying to get it open.

With a crack and a hiss the baseboard heater along the floor broke loose from the wall. Then the long pipe inside quickly pulled itself free and started floating in the air.

"Oh, my God," the man said. Then the pipe flew toward him and slammed through his chest, affixing him to the wall.

A second later the basement door opened, a bright blue and white light pouring into the kitchen and blinding Emmy. With a strong gust of wind the bodies of the two men were pulled into the basement, and then the door shut and the house was quiet again.

Emmy stood in a daze for a few moments, feeling light-headed and sick.

"Thank you," she slurred, bowing ungracefully. She then

poured herself a glass of wine.

*****

Several days later, Alex returned to the house. He walked through the door and entered the silent home.

"Emmy?" he asked into the quiet.

There was no response.

He walked through the rooms trying to locate her. He had seen her car in the garage so he knew she was home. Finally, he made his way upstairs and into the bedroom. He sighed when he saw the light on in the closet and the door closed.

"Guess nothing's changed," he said, defeated.

Alex opened the door and found Emmy sitting cross-legged on the floor inside with her head down, but he was instantly horrified by her appearance. She was about 10 or 15 pounds skinnier, a feat in and of itself for the already skinny Emmy. There were heavy bags and dark circles under her eyes, and her skin was gaunt and pale. She looked sick and weak.

"Oh, Emmy," he sighed, "what have you done to yourself?"

Emmy slowly lifted her head and looked at him.

"Me? I haven't done anything. I've never felt better," she slurred.

Suddenly the house began to shake.

"Emmy, don't do this. I'm back, okay? I'm home," Alex said, voice shaking.

"You left us," she answered in a deep, monotone voice.

"What do you mean by us?"

"Me and the house," she said as the house began to shake. Alex lost his balance and stumbled against the wall.

He pushed himself out into the hallway and headed to the stairs. Suddenly, the stairs flattened into a ramp and Alex slid all the way down, smashing into the wall head-first at the bottom. He tried to sit up, but the room was spinning around him. He couldn't tell if it was from hitting his head or if the house was actually spinning. He would have believed anything in that moment.

He struggled to get to his feet and tried to open the front door, but it wouldn't budge. The house was shaking wildly now, with objects falling off of every shelf, pictures falling off the walls, every dish and glass tumbling out of the kitchen cabinets.

Emmy slowly made her way to the flattened staircase. As if being held up on strings she floated down and hovered in front of Alex.

"What are you?" he screamed, still pawing at the door.

"We are the house," she answered plainly.

A moment later, Alex was lifted above the floor by an unseen force and slammed against the wall. He screamed as the force began roughly dragging him across the wall and toward the basement door. Books and knick-knacks and other items were flying around the house, some of them striking Alex.

The bright light emitted from the basement and the door flew open. With a strong gust of wind Alex was sucked down into the vortex and the door slammed shut. Silence and darkness once again fell over the house.

With a blink and a shake of her head Emmy was suddenly coherent and deeply disturbed by what had just happened as her floating body dropped back down to the floor.

"Wait, you can't do that!" she yelled. "You can't take him. Give him back!"

She ran to the basement door and began slamming her fists against it and trying to force it open.

"That wasn't supposed to happen. You can't have him. Give him back to me!" she screamed at the door. She stepped back and looked around.

"Stop doing this!" she shouted at no one. "Leave us alone and give him back!"

With a final burst of strength she let out a shrill, powerful scream and slammed into the basement door.

Finally, the door flew open again and the bright light appeared. Taking a deep breath and swallowing heavily, Emmy stepped forward. Just like the previous times, a gust of wind blew out and sucked her in. The last thing she heard was the door slamming shut behind her, and then silence.

She opened her eyes and found herself on the cold, damp cement floor of a dimly lit room that looked like a wine cellar. She slowly stood up and looked around her. People wearing dark hooded robes surrounded her. There were people of all ages in the room. There was a middle-aged couple and an elderly couple, a single older man, and two couples with what looked to be teenaged children. They all stared at her with pale, emaciated faces and dark eyes. The man from the older couple stepped forward.

"You were supposed to feed the house, but you became unstable unusually quickly," he said. "Sooner or later they all become unstable, and then they come here with us, but it usually happens after a few years. We control the house, you see. It feeds off of us."

"What do you want from me?" Emmy asked.

"Your power," the man's wife answered plainly. "Your life force. You will feed the house with us, with all of us. We are the house."

"We are the house," all of the other people in the room repeated together.

One voice stood out to Emmy. She looked over in the corner and saw the dead, empty eyes of Alex, staring off into the distance underneath his dark hood.

"No," Emmy muttered, her voice shaking and tears welling in her eyes. "No, you can't do this."

The older couple stepped forward and each of them gently placed a hand on Emmy's shoulders. The last thing she remembered was a feeling of peace and safety. Her mind was blank and her body relaxed. She was calm.

"We are the house," she said.

THE INVALID

Pete looked out the living room window at the house next door. An elderly couple lived there, but Pete and his wife, Andrea, hadn't really seen them or met them since moving in about five years ago. But today, for the first time, Pete caught a glimpse of the female half of the couple. She had short curly hair that was almost completely gray, and she wore thick glasses with red frames.

"What are you staring at?" Andrea said as she walked into the living room.

"I've finally seen our neighbor!" he answered. "Check it out. It's the old woman – still no sign of her husband, though."

Andrea plopped down on the couch next to him and stared out the window.

"This is ridiculous," she said. "We've been here for five years and we haven't said a thing to them. We should go over there. We need to ask them about taking down that dead tree that's right on the property line anyway."

"I guess it's now or never," Pete answered.

The two of them got up from the couch and headed outside. Next door, the neighbor was milling about in the overgrown backyard. It looked like no one had maintained the landscaping in years. As they began to cross over the property line, Pete cleared his throat.

The woman looked up, startled.

"Hello there," Pete said with a smile. "I'm Pete and this is my wife, Andrea. We live next door. We haven't met you yet so we thought we'd come over and say hello."

"Oh!" exclaimed the woman. "How lovely, it's so nice to meet you. I'm Marci."

She reached her arm out and shook Pete's hand.

"Sorry to barge over here like this but we figured it would be the perfect time to say hello and talk to you about that dead tree right over there," Andrea said, pointing behind them.

"Yes, that tree needs to go," Marci said. "We just haven't gotten around to it."

"Great, so we're in agreement," Pete said. "How about we have it taken down for you? It would be no problem."

"That would be wonderful, thank you so much," Marci said with a smile. "Things like that are so difficult for me to handle. I don't have my husband to take care of those things for me anymore."

"I'm so sorry," Andrea said. "Has he...passed on?"

"No," Marci said with a chuckle. "He's right inside, but I'm afraid you won't see much of him. He hasn't even been outside in years. He's an invalid. I take care of him."

Andrea and Pete paused awkwardly at her odd word choice.

"Well, sorry to hear that," Pete said. "If you guys ever need help with anything, we'd be glad to help you out."

"That's so nice of you," Marci said. "It's good to know I have such a lovely couple living next door. You'll have to come over sometime for cookies. Richard can't get enough of them so I'm constantly baking them."

"How sweet," Andrea said with a smile. "You seem very devoted to him. He's lucky to have you."

"Oh, yes," Marci said with a grin. "Now if you'll excuse me I have to head back in to fix dinner."

"Okay, well it was very nice meeting you," Andrea said.

"Yeah, and don't worry about that tree, we'll take care of it," Pete added.

Marci smiled and slowly walked back inside.

Andrea and Pete turned and walked back to their property.

"Well, that wasn't so bad," Pete said with relief. "She actually seems pretty nice."

"Yeah, too bad about her husband, though," Andrea added. "That's a shame. We should do something nice to help her out. Maybe I'll go find out Richard's favorite dinner and make it for them."

"Wow, that's really nice of you," Pete said. "I'll bet Marci would appreciate it. We really are going for the Neighbor of the Year award, aren't we?"

"Well, I'm certainly not going for second place," Andrea said, grinning.

*****

Inside her house, Marci walked over to the den where Richard was lying on the couch. He was struggling and trying to get up, mumbling and attempting to speak.

"Now, now, dear, that won't do," Marci said. "You need to be calm. You know what happens when you get too worked up."

Marci picked up a bag from the coffee table and reached inside, pulling out a syringe. She carefully got it prepared as Richard eyed the needle and started struggling harder.

"Don't worry, sweetheart, you won't feel a thing," she said calmly. "We've done this hundreds of times. You know what to expect."

She leaned over him and grabbed one of his arms while he continued to flail about.

"You need to keep still, dear," Marci said through gritted teeth. "I can't give you your medicine if you don't stop squirming."

Richard started to wail loudly, trying to form words but his mouth failing him.

Marci reached behind her and grabbed a belt from the table and quickly attached his arm to one of the legs of the coffee table.

"Always have to do this the hard way," Marci said with a scowl. "You know I'm doing this for you. You know I can't be without you. But I can't see you hurt. You need to take your medicine!"

She quickly plunged the needle into his arm as he let out a pained howl. Within seconds he was calming down. His body fell slack and still as his eyes drooped shut.

"There we go. Isn't that better?" Marci said. "It's just easier this way."

She stood back up and walked into the kitchen, not noticing Andrea standing just next to the open window, eyes wide and mouth agape, with her hand still raised to knock on the front door.

*****

"Pete, our neighbor is crazy! She drugs her husband and is keeping him immobile on the couch!"

"Is that you, mom?" Pete said with a smirk, his head leaning into the refrigerator.

"Pete, come on," Andrea sighed. "This is serious."

"It definitely sounds serious," Pete answered, taking out some leftovers for dinner.

"Well, then listen!" Andrea yelled, fear in her eyes.

Pete stopped what he was doing and looked her over.

"Wow, you are serious," he said.

"I went over there. I was going to ask what I could cook for them, remember? And she was, she had a…" Andrea couldn't even finish her sentence without breaking down.

"What did she do?" Pete said, walking over to her and wrapping his arms around her.

"She injected him with something that knocked him out. She's got him on a couch in the living room. She doesn't let him move, get up, walk, anything!" she said, frantic. "He was trying to get up, too, and she tied him down with a belt. Pete, I think she's keeping him on the verge of death for no reason."

Pete had no words. He stared at Andrea with terror in his eyes.

"What…what are you saying?" he sputtered.

"She's evil," Andrea breathed.

*****

The next day, Pete decided they would have to do a little more investigating before jumping to conclusions. He wanted to see the situation next door for himself.

Andrea pulled him over to the neighbor's house late that night and they peeked in through the living room window, just as she had yesterday. Richard was there lying on the couch. He didn't even look conscious. He was still, barely breathing, mouth agape and eyes fluttering under his eyelids. It seemed like a frantic, nightmare state that he couldn't escape.

"Jesus…" Pete exhaled, shaking his head.

"We need to figure out a way inside. We need to help him," Andrea said.

"How? We should just call the police, we can't do anything," Pete said.

"Oh, yeah, they're really going to respond well to this," she snapped back, raising her hand up to her ear like she was holding a phone. "'Yeah, hi, police? We were spying on our neighbors and learned that an elderly man spends all day lying on the couch. We assume his wife is evil because we saw her give him medication.' What do they have to go on?"

"They have to at least come check it out," Pete countered.

"And then what?" she said. "Throw him into a nursing home? He doesn't need one. He's fine. We need to get him off the drugs and back to his senses."

Andrea started walking around the house, trying every window to see if any were open.

"Andrea!" Pete hissed. "Are you crazy? Stop it!"

Andrea kept trying each window. She made her way onto the back deck and found the window over the kitchen sink open and waiting for her. She pulled out a pocket knife and started cutting the screen.

"Why do you have a knife?" Pete rasped, still trying to stay quiet despite his panic.

Andrea kept cutting. Once she had made a sizable hole she ripped through the rest of the screen and started climbing through the window.

"Oh, my God," Pete sighed as he watched Andrea wiggle her way through the tiny opening.

She cringed as she banged her knee on the faucet while trying to maneuver her body inside. Pete started making his way in behind her just as she hopped down to her feet. She paused, listening. Hearing nothing she walked toward the living room. Pete walked up behind her and she silently gestured toward Richard on the couch, signaling with her hands that they would need to pick him up. Pete took a deep breath and nodded, and the two of them walked over to him. Andrea grabbed his legs, Pete grabbed under his shoulders and together they lifted him up.

As they ambled back to the entryway, Andrea slowly lowered Richard's legs so she could open the front door. The door made an obnoxiously loud creaking noise as it opened, and they both froze in place waiting and listening. Hearing nothing again, Andrea scooped up Richard's legs and they carried him out the door. Pete eased the door shut with his foot as they went.

After what felt like hours later but was really just minutes, the couple was back on their property with Richard in their arms. He had awoken somewhat and was muttering and trying to move. Andrea tried to softly calm him down.

"Don't worry, Richard. It's okay. We're friends," she said softly. "We're going to help you. We're going to make sure you're okay. You're going to stay with us until the drugs get out of your system then we're going to get you help."

He tried to mumble something but Andrea shushed him.

"It's okay, just be calm," she said.

She opened the back door to their house and they carried him inside, placing him softly on their living room couch.

"Sorry to give you another couch, partner, but you're a bit too much for us to carry up the stairs," Pete said.

Andrea adjusted the pillow behind Richard's head and

placed a blanket over him.

"There you go," she said, reassuringly, "you're going to be just fine. Just get some sleep and we'll take care of you in the morning."

Andrea and Pete smiled down at Richard as he finally seemed to calm down. They both turned and made their way upstairs to their room to try and get a few hours of sleep.

*****

Hours later, Andrea woke to the sun streaming through her bedroom window. She sighed lightly and smiled, until she noticed an odd sound coming from next to her.

She glanced to her left to find Richard, very much mobile and active, sitting on top of her husband and holding a large knife, plunging it repeatedly into Pete's chest. Richard began laughing hysterically as he continued to stab Pete's lifeless body.

Andrea screamed at the top of her lungs and rolled off of the bed, crawling into the corner of the room. Richard barely paused to look at her through his repeated stabbing of Pete. Behind him, Andrea noticed Marci standing there.

"You couldn't have just left us alone," Marci said.

"What the hell is going on?!" Andrea screamed. "What is wrong with him?!"

"What do you think?" Marci asked. "Why do you think I was keeping him sedated? He's dangerous."

Marci slowly walked forward and put her hand on Richard's shoulder. He stopped stabbing and sat panting.

"I love him," Marci said. "He's my husband. I don't want to live without him. But no one would understand him. They'd take him away from me. They'd leave me alone. I had to keep him with me, and sedating him was the only way."

Marci ran her hand through Richard's hair as he closed his eyes and sighed, leaning into the touch.

"He means everything to me," Marci continued, "and I can't live without him. You understand that now, right?"

Andrea stared at her, wide-eyed and frozen in fear. She then noticed Richard was now staring at her with a crooked smile.

"You should have just left us alone," Marci said as she backed away.

The last image Andrea had was of Richard hopping on top of her and slamming his knife into her chest while Marci smiled softly behind him, holding a syringe.

HIT AND RUN

"Brett, wake up! What's taking you so long with that brake job?"

Brett snapped back to reality, standing under a car that was raised up on the lift in the garage.

"Almost done," he said quickly as he finished up. As he began lowering the car back down to the floor he let out a heavy sigh and ran his hand through his long hair.

Brett had been working at Speedy Jack's auto repair shop for the past 10 years, and he basically hated every aspect of it: the customers, his boss, his fellow employees, the lousy pay, being constantly covered in grease. It all made him angry.

In fact, everything seemed to be making him angry lately. He wasn't normally a chipper and cheerful guy, but for the past month or so he had been feeling downright homicidal. It was as if anything could set him off.

Suddenly, one of his younger coworkers tip-toed by him. He appeared to be sneaking up on another worker. The boy reached back and slapped the unaware worker across the back of his head as hard as he could.

"Ah! What the hell?" the man barked. The rest of the shop erupted into laughter.

"Hit and run!" yelled the attacker as he ran away.

The victim rubbed the back of his head while he chuckled and shook his head.

"You better run," he said, shaking a finger. "You're next, you little punk."

Brett rolled his eyes and sighed again, climbing into the car he had worked on and driving it out of the garage. As he drove around to the front of the shop he noticed the attacker standing outside smoking and laughing with another co-worker. Ryan was the kid's name, Brett remembered. What a little jackass he was.

Without realizing it, Brett started speeding up. The image of him slamming the car into Ryan and pinning his body to the wall of the shop briefly flashed across his eyes.

He blinked several times and shook his head as he pulled the car into a parking space.

"Dangerous thoughts, man," he said out loud to himself as he walked back inside the shop to hand the keys off to the owner.

It was near closing time and everyone was milling about the shop, cleaning up their stations and putting away paperwork. Jack, the owner, came out from his office and stretched.

"Okay, losers, get out of my shop so I can go home and drink," he said.

The crew said their goodbyes to each other and started filing out into the parking lot. Brett had just pulled his keys out of his pocket when he felt a sharp slap on the back of his head.

"Hit and run!" Ryan yelled as he ran away laughing hysterically. The rest of the group laughed and shook their heads as they got into their trucks. Brett stood still, seething.

"Hey, Brett, you okay?" one of the guys asked. "Did he hit something important? You ain't moving."

Brett's chest began heaving. He saw nothing but red, and flexed his hands into fists. Then, he suddenly began to laugh. It was a light chuckle at first that grew in intensity.

The guys who were left in the parking lot slowly started backing away to their trucks. Brett was laughing maniacally now and it was frightening them. They all drove away as Brett stayed behind, laughing loudly to himself in the parking lot.

As quickly as he had started he stopped laughing and looked into the distance. He saw that Ryan had gone across the street to the liquor store and was walking back toward the shop holding a case of beer.

Brett narrowed his eyes and smiled darkly as he climbed into his truck.

As soon as he started the engine he whipped out of the parking space and blew across the street, narrowly avoiding a collision with a passing car. Ryan looked up when he heard the commotion just as he was about to cross the street. He quickly realized that a truck was speeding right toward him.

"Whoa, man, what the hell?!" he yelled out as he dropped the beer and took off running. The truck picked up speed and continued aiming right for him.

"What are you doing? Stop it! Leave me alone!" Ryan screamed as he started running along the road.

Brett floored it, his truck surging forward and staying right on Ryan's tail, even driving on the wrong side of the road. Ryan looked ahead of him in a panic, screaming for someone to help him and trying to find a way out as he bobbed and weaved around the road.

"Okay, that's enough," Brett muttered to himself and the truck slowed to a stop, its headlights still focused on Ryan.

Ryan stopped running and bent over himself, hands on his knees, gasping for air and panting.

"You…you crazy son of a bitch," he gasped. "What is your problem, man?"

Brett rolled down his window and poked his head out. Ryan squinted to see through the light.

"….Brett?" he said.

"Hit and run," Brett answered plainly as he slammed on the gas and plowed his truck into Ryan. The boy's body was tossed up over the windshield and slammed down on the tailgate before rolling off into the street.

Brett hit the brakes, jerked the truck around and barreled forward, running over the body to ensure it wouldn't be getting up again.

He then drove back into the parking lot of the liquor store and pulled up alongside the abandoned case of beer, opening his door to reach down and grab it. Then he sped off toward home.

*****

The next morning, Brett woke up with an incredible feeling of euphoria. He stretched and smiled wide at the sun pouring in through the window. The events of the previous night were still swimming in his brain and he wanted more. He glanced over at the clock and saw it was already 11:30 a.m. He hadn't slept that well in a long time.

He was up and out of bed within minutes, heading out the door to find some brunch and whatever else might come his way. And he had no intention of going into work that day.

Brett pulled up to the local diner and strolled over to the front steps, whistling. He walked up to the entrance just as an elderly couple was exiting. He held the door open for them before waltzing inside himself.

As he sat down at the counter he pulled out his phone, noticing a lot of missed text messages and some voicemails. The texts were from his coworkers telling him about the "horrible accident" that happened the previous night and that "poor Ryan was killed." There were also several messages from his boss asking him why he wasn't at work.

Brett smiled and put his phone away as the waitress came up to him. He ordered coffee and a stack of pancakes, and then glanced up at the TV mounted to the wall. A local news reporter was retelling the events from last night, and the crew was even set up in the parking lot of the liquor store. A few locals in the diner were gasping as they listened to the details. All they knew was that a young man had been struck by a truck repeatedly, and that the truck's driver was never identified.

"How awful," said the waitress as she poured Brett's coffee.

"Yeah," he said, "some messed up people out there."

"That's for sure," she said as she walked away.

Brett grinned again.

"What the hell are you smiling so much about?" a man two seats down at the counter said suddenly.

Brett looked up and stared at him.

"Excuse me?" he said.

"You heard me," the man continued. "A kid was killed and you're grinning over there like you think it's funny. What's your problem?"

"Come on, Bill, leave it. He was probably thinking of something else," the waitress said. "Don't start something."

"That's good advice right there," Brett said as he turned back around in his stool and faced front.

"Yeah, wouldn't wanna start nothin' with me, that's for sure," Bill muttered.

Brett rolled his eyes as the waitress took Bill's order.

"I'll have a ham and cheese sandwich, and a bowl of the soup," Bill said. "And make sure it's hot this time, okay? It was lukewarm last time."

Another vision passed by Brett's eyes as the waitress walked over to the kitchen window, grabbed his pancakes and placed them in front of him.

"I'll take the check, too, actually," Brett said to her, "kind of in a hurry."

"No problem, honey," she said, heading to the cash register.

"Yeah, dude's probably headed to a funeral so he can laugh at the family or something," Bill said.

Brett quietly ate his pancakes without a word. When he was done he pulled out some cash, leaving a hefty tip for the waitress for having to put up with guys like Bill, and to make up for what he was about to do.

He took the last few sips of his coffee until the moment he was waiting for arrived and a little bell in the kitchen dinged. Bill's lunch was ready. The waitress headed into the kitchen to grab it. Brett waited a few more seconds then calmly got up out of his seat and headed to the door.

"Later, smiley," Bill said as Brett walked by.

The waitress approached with the tray of food and before she even knew what was happening, Brett grabbed the bowl of soup and flung its scalding hot contents into Bill's face.

He screamed in agony and pawed at his eyes as Brett grabbed the soup spoon and shoved it into Bill's mouth, lodging it in his throat. The waitress stood there in shock before trying to help Bill, who was gripping his throat and making choking noises. Brett continued walking out the door without even pausing.

"Hey, you get back here!" the waitress yelled after him as other customers in the restaurant started screaming.

Brett jogged over to his truck and hopped in. He started the engine and immediately pulled out of the parking lot just as a manager and a bus boy ran outside the restaurant. They might have gotten his license plate number. They also might have noticed some leftover blood still caked on his black truck, but Brett just kept driving. He was going to ride this high for as long as he possibly could.

*****

Brett decided to head back to his apartment to pick up some things. Intuition told him that he wouldn't be coming home again. He grabbed a duffle bag and a backpack and started filling them with clothes and some food.

He collected all of his credit cards, a book of matches, and his toothbrush. Then he tied his long hair back into a ponytail and put on a pair of sunglasses.

Finally, he grabbed a shoe box from under his bed and opened it. He emptied it of the cash he was saving for a new truck and stuffed it into his backpack. He took one last look at the place then walked out, locking the door behind him. A smile was plastered on his face the entire time.

"Let's have some fun," he said to himself as he started his truck and reversed out of the apartment complex.

While his truck maneuvered through the residential neighborhood he noticed a couple of young boys riding ATVs in the road coming up behind him. He stopped at a stop sign but the boys sped up and whipped around him to pass him. He glared at them as they rode by and they both flipped him their middle fingers.

"All right then," Brett said, smiling again.

He hit the gas and sped off after them. He turned on the MP3 player in his truck and started to sing along to the Misfits song that was blasting through the speakers.

The boys heard the truck quickly approaching them and looked behind them. Terrified to find out who it was behind the wheel, they desperately tried to get their ATVs to go faster. They began weaving through people's yards in an effort to dodge him.

Brett started laughing loudly between belting out song lyrics, speeding around sharp turns and never losing sight of the boys. By taking a shortcut on a side road Brett was able to cut off the boys unexpectedly. They both screamed as they saw him rapidly approaching them on a perpendicular road and veered out of his way. He was now right on their tails heading downhill.

Brett let out a high-pitched howl as he sped up. With the gas pedal floored he plowed into the boys, sending them flying off their ATVs and rolling down the rest of the hill. Brett veered around their overturned ATVs and ran over both of the boys, finishing the job. He looked around and noticed neighbors outside screaming at him and running toward the boys.

"Owwwwww!" Brett yelped again as he jerked the car around and sped out of the area. He drove straight to the highway and headed south, laughing and singing the whole way.

*****

Brett drove for three hours or so before he realized he was hungry again. He pulled off at an exit and drove through a new town trying to find a place to eat. After hitting a fast food drive-through he realized he was getting low on gas, so he drove into the gas station across the street.

He got out of the truck and headed inside to pay the cashier first. As he walked back to the pump he saw a pudgy, balding man at the next pump staring uneasily at Brett's blood-splattered truck.

Brett smiled at him and shrugged.

"Pretty big deer," he said with a chuckle.

With a relieved look on his face, the man laughed.

"Oh, yeah, I hear that. Hit a big one myself a year back," he said. "My car hasn't sounded the same since."

Brett stood next to his truck pumping gas as the other customers around him began staring at him and whispering to each other. He continued to play it cool, even whistling as he pumped, willing the gas to hurry up and get in his truck.

Suddenly he saw a woman exit the gas station with a couple of sports drinks, stopping in her tracks and staring wide-eyed at Brett and his truck. She slowly crept toward the pudgy man.

"What's wrong, Barbara?" the man said to her.

She leaned in and whispered something in his ear as the man's complexion turned pale and his eyes became as wide as hers.

Here we go, thought Brett.

The woman took out her cell phone and walked away from the pumps as she dialed. Other people started backing away slowly and getting into their cars.

"Hey, buddy," the man said nervously, "that was no deer that did that to your truck, was it?"

Brett chuckled.

"Nope, it wasn't," he said with a grin as he stopped the pump.

"You...you better just stay right there, mister," the man said, gradually backing away. "My wife's over there calling the police as we speak. We can end this civilly. Nobody else needs to get hurt here."

Brett continued grinning as he slowly approached the man, the gas nozzle still in his hand.

"Why not?" he asked. "It's fun, you should try it sometime."

Brett reached out and grabbed the man by the shoulder. He wrapped the hose around the man's neck and pulled it tight. People around him started to scream and run away. The manager of the gas station ran outside to see what all of the commotion was about and froze when he saw what was happening.

Brett pointed the nozzle at the man's face and squeezed, pouring gasoline all over him. The man choked and sputtered as Brett kicked him down to the ground. He then calmly walked back to his truck and got in.

After starting his truck Brett pulled it forward, next to the man, and tossed something out of his window before taking off.

A lighted match fell to the ground without a sound as a fireball erupted around the man and the gas pumps. As Brett sped away, he chuckled when he heard the sound of screams followed by a loud explosion.

*****

Brett chose to change direction and head west, and after several more hours of driving he decided to stop for the night. He pulled off the highway into yet another town and found a motel. He paid for the room upfront in cash, claiming he had no credit cards on him. The man behind the desk shrugged and took his money, handing him a key to his room.

He slept soundly again that night, dreaming of explosions, fire, and scorched flesh. He woke up before the sun, ecstatic to look out the window and see rain washing the blood off of his truck. After a shower and some food from his backpack he hit the road again.

But he was itching for more fun.

He decided to explore the town a little more. After getting more gas for his truck, discreetly this time, he drove around a few side streets. Finding nothing of interest he made his way back to the main road to head to the highway again.

Suddenly he heard loud noises coming up behind him. He glanced in his rearview mirror and saw a group of five men on loud, neon-colored sport bikes closing in quickly.

He sighed and sped up slightly, turning his music back on, but the bikes continued their assault until they were right on his tail. They weaved back and forth, trying to get him to speed up or get out of the way. The men were so close that he was certain if they reached out they could grab his truck.

Giving them one more chance, he sped up his truck again. The men only closed in more, creating a line behind his truck and revving their engines. One of them even popped a wheelie and displayed his middle finger to Brett's rearview mirror.

Without even a second of hesitation, Brett slammed on his brakes and jerked the steering wheel to the side, causing his truck to drift sideways along the road before stopping. The five bikers slammed right into the side of his truck, their bodies thrown clear through the air before crashing down on the pavement.

Brett laughed and began singing along to his music again as he sped forward and ran over all of them.

Then it was back to the highway, this time heading south again.

*****

Brett continued driving for most of the day, smiling and singing along to his loud music. He was so engulfed in the songs that he didn't immediately hear the sound of sirens behind him.

He was snapped back to reality when a police cruiser pulled up right behind him with its lights flashing and siren blaring.

After a moment, Brett decided to start singing again and ignore the growing amount of red and blue lights flashing behind him. One of the cops might have even said "pull over" through a megaphone, but he pretended not to hear. He continued driving until he saw a blockade of cop cars ahead of him.

Brett floored the gas pedal and approached at full speed, singing the entire time, loudly and enthusiastically. He didn't notice that the officers outside of the cars had their guns drawn, and he certainly didn't hear the multiple bullets that shot through his windshield and struck him in his head and chest.

Brett's body slumped over the steering wheel and the truck veered off to the side of the road, crashing into a tree.

Officers sprinted over to the truck, shouting at him to put his hands up. One of them ripped open the door of the truck as they all aimed their guns at Brett.

He was unresponsive, still slumped over the steering wheel. An officer reached over to touch his neck, feeling for a pulse. He felt none, so he pulled Brett's lifeless body up into a sitting position again. He had several bullet holes in his head and chest.

A smile was still plastered on his face.

FRAN MAGLIONE

THE DRONE

Eric excitedly ran down to the mailroom of his apartment building one Saturday afternoon, fingers crossed that he'd see a package there waiting for him. Sure enough, there it was in a pile of other packages on the floor: a brand new drone that he'd been saving up to buy for almost an entire year. He grabbed the package and bounded back up the stairs to his eighth floor apartment.

His roommate, Nick, was exactly where he left him: sitting on the couch playing a video game wearing sweatpants and an old t-shirt.

"Dude, it's here!" Eric yelled happily as he tore open the box.

"Sweet," Nick replied, uninterested as he focused his attention on battling zombies on the screen.

After a couple of hours of prepping it, charging the battery and reading over the instructions, Eric was ready to take the drone out for a test fly. He pulled Nick away from the TV screen and the two of them walked across the street to the park.

"Okay, man, now check this out," Eric said as the drone suddenly came to life and took off, lights flashing on each of its four arms.

"Whoa, not bad," Nick said. "It flies really smoothly."

"Yeah, it's great," Eric said. "It's easy to fly, and it can even go as high as the top of our apartment building."

Eric maneuvered the remote control in his hands and the drone started to lift higher and higher until it was above the tops of the trees. Nick stared up at it in awe.

"And that's not even the best part," Eric boasted. "It has a built-in video camera. It's recording everything it's seeing right now."

"That's awesome," Nick chuckled. "Can I give it a try?"

The two took turns flying the drone for another hour or so until the battery started to die. After a fairly rough landing that Nick assured Eric he would continue practicing, they brought the drone back inside and hooked it up to Eric's computer.

The first video footage they saw was fairly sharp and steady, showcasing the vibrant green shade of the trees. They even got footage of the roof of the apartment building, laughing at the abundance of bird droppings and old beer cans that were up there.

"This thing is great," Nick said. "Charge it up and we'll take it outside again later."

The rest of the day continued with the boys alternating between flying the drone and sitting in front of the TV while it charged on the desk. Finally, content with their progress that day and full of enough beer to subdue an elephant, the two headed to their respective rooms to go to sleep.

*****

The next morning, Eric woke up and headed to the kitchen to make coffee only to find that Nick was already up, continuing his video game on the couch. Momentarily shocked by his roommate's out-of-character early rise, he shrugged and started the coffee maker.

"We should take the drone down to the river today," Eric said. "We could probably fly it all the way across to the other shore."

"Yeah, definitely," Nick replied. "Hey, remember that time

we threw Frank's sneaker in that tree across the street? I wonder if we caught it in our footage from yesterday. I didn't think to look."

Eric laughed out loud at the memory.

"I forgot about that!" he said. "Let's take another look. Then we can send a screen grab to Frank."

The two went over to the desk and hooked the drone back up to Eric's computer. They opened up yesterday's videos, but were surprised to find there was a new video saved. Its timestamp read 3:42 a.m.

"What's that?" Nick asked.

"I have no idea," Eric said. "We were both asleep then. Maybe it malfunctioned and filmed the wall by accident or something."

He clicked on the video and saw that it was two hours long.

"How is that possible?" Eric asked. "The battery only lasts an hour."

They watched the video together, trying to decipher the dark, grainy footage. It was clearly taken in the dark and indoors.

"Was the drone flying around the apartment?" Nick asked, his voice starting to shake.

The footage weaved through the apartment and over to Eric's closed bedroom door. An unseen force opened the door and the drone flew inside. Then it hovered over Eric's bed, filming his sleeping form. The footage continued like that as the drone floated perfectly still over Eric.

After a few moments Eric fast-forwarded the footage and they saw that the drone had filmed him sleeping for the rest of the video. Finally, at the two-hour mark, the footage ended.

Suddenly, Eric started to laugh.

"You jerk," he said, looking at Nick.

Nick was just staring at him, eyes wide.

"You were doing that, weren't you?" Eric said, still chuckling. "You almost had me, man. That was a good one. But how did you get the battery to last so long, and get it to hover so steadily over me?"

Nick just continued to stare at Eric.

"I didn't do that," he said plainly.

"Come on, I'm not stupid," Eric said, growing impatient. "Just tell me how you did it. I'm not mad, it was a good prank! You really almost had me."

"Dude, I'm serious! I didn't do that!" Nick yelled back.

Eric sighed and got up.

"Whatever, man. I'm going to have some cereal then we can go fly this thing some more."

*****

After another day of flying the drone the two cut the evening short and went to bed. The next morning they both headed off to work – Eric to the local bookstore and Nick to the supermarket.

When Eric returned home at the end of his shift, he decided to take a look at the drone's video footage again before Nick got home. He hooked it up and was about to click on the video when he spotted yet another new video saved. This one was from 2:16 a.m.

Eric sighed.

"No wonder he's always tired. He wakes up in the middle of the night to prank me."

He played the video, but this time was surprised to find the drone approaching Nick's room instead of his. The door was opened in the same fashion, and the drone hovered inside just above Nick's sleeping body. This time the video lasted three hours.

Too engrossed in the terrifying and confusing footage, Eric didn't hear Nick come in until he was right behind him. The sound of Nick dropping his things heavily behind him snapped him back to reality. He turned around to see Nick staring at the screen, eyes wide and frightened.

"What the hell is that?" Nick shouted to Eric. "I told you I didn't film you that night. Stop trying to mess with me to teach me a lesson!"

Eric stood up, holding his hands out in a pacifying stance.

"Nick, I didn't do this," he said. "Look, there's obviously something wrong with this drone. Maybe if I box it back up perfectly they'll let me return it. It doesn't have any scratches or dings on it yet."

Nick stood still, looking Eric up and down, mistrust in his eyes. Eric did the same. The two silently parted ways and didn't speak the rest of the evening, only occasionally exchanging suspicious glances.

That night the boys both locked their bedroom doors. Nick even pushed his dresser in front of his.

"Let's see him get in here now," Nick chuckled.

The two of them each lay awake on their beds and stared at the ceiling, unable to sleep. Finally, an hour or two later, they had both drifted off.

*****

The next morning, Eric awoke to what sounded like Nick pushing his dresser away from his door. Then he heard Nick's door open, so he quickly got up and opened his door.

The boys stood in their doorways, staring at each other. Finally, Eric ran over to the desk, Nick close behind him. Eric hooked up the drone and looked at the videos that were saved. There was another new one from the middle of the night.

They exchanged frightened looks, and then Eric hesitantly clicked the video.

The footage was dark and grainy again, but it didn't appear to be in their apartment anymore.

"Where is it?" Nick whispered.

Eric stayed silent, eyes glued to the computer screen.

The drone was hovering around what looked like someone else's living room. It then flew into a bedroom where an older man and woman slept in a large bed. The drone hovered over them until the man opened his eyes.

"What's this?" the man asked, as the woman next to him began to wake up.

Then the couple looked over at something just to the right of the camera and their eyes grew wide. They both began to scream, and then the video ended.

Eric and Nick sat quietly in front of the computer, neither of them moving a muscle.

"What did we just watch?" Eric breathed.

"It's got to be a joke," Nick said. "It has to be. It has to be some sort of prank by the guys who made this thing. They could be watching us right now, laughing at us."

Eric looked at the drone sitting innocently on his desk. Suddenly he stood up and grabbed it, walking toward the window.

"I've had enough of this," he said. "I don't care how much this cost. It ends now."

Eric opened the window and pulled out the screen. He then picked up the drone and heaved it out the window as Nick watched from behind him. The drone spun as it fell the eight floors then smashed into the pavement, pieces of it scattering all around.

Without another word, Eric and Nick got ready for work.

*****

That night the two had felt more comfortable in the apartment and were able to fall asleep easily. The drone was gone and they could move on, trying to forget the video they had seen, so they both left their doors unlocked that night.

Eric woke up with a start when he heard a scream in the middle of the night. He sat up in his bed and listened. It sounded like Nick screaming. After a few moments the screaming stopped.

He's probably having a nightmare, Eric thought. This whole ordeal had been a little creepy.

He lay back down in his bed and tried to go to sleep until a dull whirring sound startled him awake again. He sat up and looked at his bedroom door, which was open now, and gasped in terror.

The drone was slowly hovering into his bedroom, its bright light blinding him.

"No, this can't be happening," he whimpered, clutching his

blankets tight. "I destroyed you."

He then noticed a figure standing behind the drone and his eyes widened.

Eric's scream pierced through the quiet room until the only sound left was the low buzzing of the drone.

FRAN MAGLIONE

LEAVE

The loudest thunderclap Bobby had ever heard exploded seemingly right above his head, ripping him from a sound sleep.

Flashes of lightning filled his bedroom casting jarring shadows on the walls. He rolled over and looked at the clock. It read 5:47 a.m.

"Great," he sighed, "I can't even sleep in on a Saturday morning."

He cuddled back into his pillow and tried to drift back to sleep while the thunder continued rumbling in the background, exploding so loudly every so often that he'd jerk back awake. A strong gust of wind blew in through the open window, tossing the drapes around. The rain relentlessly pounded on the roof of the house.

The constant barrage of thunder and lightning kept him awake for another 10 minutes or so until the storm finally drifted far away enough for Bobby to sleep.

Hours later he slowly woke to the sound of whispering in his ear.

"Leave," a voice hissed, over and over. "Leave."

His eyes opened as he gasped and froze in place in his bed. He held his breath and listened closely around him. The sun was up and birds were singing – the storm long gone. He heard no voices, but his room practically buzzed with negative energy. It felt as though the storm had brought in something that was very angry.

Bobby shuddered and got out of bed. Andrew would be over to visit in a couple of hours and he figured he should at least be showered and dressed. Still half asleep, he stumbled down the stairs to his kitchen, desperate for coffee.

The house was eerily silent, and he quickly brewed his coffee while trying to ignore the feeling he had of being watched. As he filled his mug, a small dark figure moved along his peripheral vision. He glanced over and saw a shadow floating along the hallway toward the front door, out of sight.

Bobby turned the corner and looked down the hallway, seeing nothing.

When the coffee maker stopped percolating he poured himself a cup, and then he took a long sip of his coffee and sighed. Around him, the house whispered.

"Leave."

*****

When Andrew pulled up to the house he was surprised to see Bobby sitting outside on the steps. He stepped out of his car and approached with a smirk on his face.

"I get a formal greeting party when I arrive now? Wow, I feel so special!" he laughed as he leaned over and kissed Bobby hello.

"Don't flatter yourself, the house is haunted," Bobby replied as he stood up to give Andrew a hug.

"Haunted? What makes you say that?" Andrew asked with a chuckle.

"Oh, you know, disembodied spirits, creepy voices, shadows wandering the halls, et cetera," Bobby said, sighing.

"Guess we'll have to talk to the landlord," Andrew laughed. He took Bobby's hand and pulled him up off the steps and guided him back toward the house. Bobby hesitated at the entrance, though, afraid to walk inside.

Andrew sighed and gently pulled Bobby into the house.

"It's okay, nothing is going to hurt you. Now, show me all of the scary —" Andrew couldn't even finish his sentence before he felt a gust of wind blow by him carrying a whispering voice. A small shadow figure appeared on the wall in front of them and immediately vanished.

"Well, there you go," Bobby said.

"That voice definitely sounds pretty disembodied," Andrew said, looking around the room. "Is it just one spirit here or are there several?"

Bobby paused and squinted his eyes as he looked around, then he held his finger in the air as if he were testing the direction of the wind. He then walked around the first floor of the house peering into each room, examining every surface, and placing his ear against the walls, knocking on them as he listened. He did this across the entire first floor of the house. He then went to a drawer in the kitchen and took out a flashlight. After switching on the flashlight he got down on all fours and peered underneath every piece of furniture.

When he was done with his performance he stood back up, brushed off his pants and sighed, rolling his eyes and glaring at Andrew.

"I have no freaking idea, idiot," he said.

"Wow, that was commitment to a physical comedy bit," Andrew said, slowing clapping his hands as Bobby bowed. "Now if you're done being a smartass let's figure out what we're dealing with here."

Andrew walked into the middle of the room.

"Hello? Whoever is in here, say something," he called out.

The gust of wind returned and the whispering began again.

"What is it saying?" Andrew asked.

"It's telling us to leave," Bobby said with a frown. "Whatever it is, it's pretty rude. The rent in this place is killer for this neighborhood. I'm not going anywhere."

"You're not leaving just because some voice calmly whispered it to you," Andrew said. "The least it can do is growl it menacingly at night or something."

"Don't give it ideas!" Bobby yelled.

"Leave!" growled the spirit.

"See? Now that's better," Andrew said, nodding.

"Would you stop it?" Bobby snapped at Andrew. He turned to look at the rest of the house. "Whoever is here, please get out of my house. I have nothing you want or need so just leave us be."

The house shook lightly before stopping almost immediately.

"That was pretty pitiful," Andrew said.

"Maybe the ghost is a child?" Bobby said. "Yes! It's a poor little child. He's probably just scared because we're in his house and he doesn't know who we are."

"Do you know anything about who the previous owners of this house were?" Andrew asked. "Maybe a family used to live here who lost a child, and he's still here somewhere."

"We need to find out who he is and see if we can help him," Bobby said. "Then he can be at peace and pass over to the next life or whatever."

Andrew walked over to the desk in the den and turned the computer on.

"Let's do a little research," he said as Bobby pulled up a chair next to him. "Maybe we can find out who lived here before."

After a few minutes of searching they learned that the house wasn't very old, and many tenants had rented it during that short time. Several of them appeared to be families with children, but a few searches on the names of the children didn't turn up any obituaries or gruesome news stories.

"Okay, so maybe it's not a child," Andrew said.

Bobby yawned and stretched in his chair before standing up.

"Let's get out of here. Haunted or not I'm still hungry. We'll deal with this after I've had an omelet and a Bloody Mary."

The two walked out to Andrew's car and drove to the diner. When they arrived they sat in their favorite booth in the corner. As they sat waiting for their food, Bobby stared at his drink with a despondent look on his face and played with the straw.

"I guess you're probably a little distracted right now," Andrew said.

"I don't like the idea of something trying to kick me out of my own home. We've been here too long to have to move again. I just want to stop moving around. And what if it's nothing? Maybe it's just a wild hangover. Or maybe I'm losing my mind," Bobby said as he cradled his head in his hands.

"Well, if you're going crazy then so am I because I was there, too," Andrew said. "There is something in that house and we're going to take care of it. Don't worry. We'll do this together. We're a team, remember? Always have been."

Bobby looked up at Andrew through his hands. He slowly lowered them from his face and smiled.

"Thank you," he said.

"Of course," Andrew said. "I mean, I have to deal with these ghosts, too."

The two of them chuckled at the booth as the waitress brought their food over.

*****

As they drove back to the house, Andrew turned the car off of the main road. Bobby watched out the window, confused until he noticed they were approaching the library.

"I don't even have a library card," Bobby said with a laugh.

"Of course you don't," Andrew said as he rolled his eyes. "I happen to have one, as the smarter and more well-read of the two of us."

Bobby lightly slapped his arm as they parked the car and walked to the front door.

"Okay, professor. Where to?" Bobby asked.

Andrew led them toward the back of the library to the reference section. They walked by the history books, weaved around the science aisles, and continued walking farther back. Once they reached the Spiritual/New Wave section, Bobby raised an eyebrow.

"Don't give me that look," Andrew snapped at him. "There just might be something here to help you."

After contemplating the books on display, Andrew reached up and plucked <u>A Comprehensive History of Dark Magic</u> off one of the top shelves. He also grabbed a reference book explaining supernatural entities, and just for fun he picked up the book <u>So Your House is Haunted</u>.

Bobby tried to contain his laughter.

"This is ridiculous, you have got to be kidding," he said.

Andrew started walking up to the front desk with the books and his library card in hand, a very serious expression on his face.

"Better get moving," he said over his shoulder, "we have a lot of reading to do."

*****

The two sat at Bobby's kitchen table with mugs of coffee and the books open in front of them, occasionally laughing uncontrollably at the verbiage used.

"Listen to this," Andrew laughed as he started reading the pages of the dark magic book. "Necromancy is the art of controlling the spirits of the dead. But be warned that this is actually a very dangerous practice."

The two men broke into a fit of laughter.

"Do they really think so? Controlling the dead isn't safe?" Bobby laughed. "Something tells me the guy who wrote this tried once and it didn't end so well."

"He probably wasn't doing it right," Andrew added. "The occult isn't for just anyone, you know."

Suddenly the temperature of the house dropped several degrees and the whispering voice came back.

"Leave," it hissed again.

"Yeah, yeah, we hear you," Andrew said, waving his hand. "Settle down."

"What about this?" Bobby asked, pointing to a page in one of the books. "It says here we could sacrifice a goat to summon a spirit."

"Where are we going to get a goat?" Andrew asked. "Are there any 24-hour goat marts around here?"

Bobby stopped to think for a moment.

"Didn't your friend Ally's aunt have a farm? Maybe she has goats."

Andrew started to laugh again.

"You're too much," he said, shaking his head.

Shadows began appearing on the walls around them again, floating around the room in a dizzying display. They seemed more agitated now as the men continued reading through the books.

"Getting nervous, buddy?" Andrew said into the room. "Do you think we're going to find something to get rid of you?"

"He's just worried that we're going to go get some goats," Bobby said. "He'll be in trouble then."

The two started laughing hysterically again at the table as the spirits continued twirling around the room. One of the shadows knocked a couple of plates off a shelf in the dining room and they fell to the floor with a crash. Bobby gasped.

"Those were antiques," he said as she slowly walked over to the broken shards on the floor and knelt down beside them. "I've had them forever. They were such a great find from nineteenth century France."

Andrew walked over and knelt down next to him placing a hand on his shoulder. Bobby was holding the jagged pieces in his hands and sighing deeply.

"I'm so sorry, Bobby," Andrew said, turning his head toward the ceiling. "Okay, a line has been crossed now. You can't just destroy a valuable personal relic that means a lot to someone."

Andrew stood up and raised his arms above his head.

"I'm ending this now," he said. "We've mocked you enough, and you just ruined the game for us anyway. I am lowering our protective barrier. You may show yourself to us now."

With a wave of his arms a figure in a bright white cloak appeared in front of the two men. His form slowly took shape into a man.

"Archangel Michael, we meet again," Andrew said with a bored sigh. "It's been a long time since you were last able to find us."

"It was not for lack of trying," Michael said. "Your magic is powerful, but not powerful enough to block me out completely."

"Evidently not since you were still able to heartlessly smash these beautiful plates I bought centuries ago," Bobby said with a sneer.

"Oh, like you really bought those," Andrew said, rolling his eyes.

"Regardless of whether I paid for them or not they were sentimental to me," Bobby said, standing up and turning to the glowing white figure. "So, you finally found us again."

"You managed to evade me for quite a while this time. It took me many long years to locate you, but no matter where you both run to I will always find you eventually," Michael said. "We will always find you."

Michael stepped forward and raised his glowing hands.

"It is time for you to return to the depths of Hell from whence you came," he said.

"Not this again," Andrew sighed.

"You've been trying to get rid of us for centuries," Bobby said. "What makes you think you've got us now?"

"You're growing weaker," Michael said. "Demons that have no power to feed upon grow weak, while we in the heavens continue to grow strong."

Andrew wordlessly stepped forward and threw his hands in front of him. Bursts of light shot out of his hands and blasted straight through Michael. The angel was violently thrown backward and crashed into the wall.

"That is a myth," Andrew said plainly.

Bobby walked over and took his place beside Andrew. Together they launched their attacks against Michael, tossing him around the room like a rag doll. Other angels appeared in the room attempting to help Michael, but the two dark angels were more powerful than they had anticipated.

The battle raged on for several moments longer until the archangel grew impatient. He stood in front of them and raised his arms.

"You cannot defeat us!" he bellowed at Bobby and Andrew. "You know this. You will never have more power than us. Stop this madness and leave this place forever."

"Well, we may not have the power to destroy you completely but we can certainly keep you out of our hair for a while. You see, dear Michael, the lords of darkness have no desire to leave this planet anytime soon. In fact, we quite like it here and intend to stay indefinitely. However, this sort of interruption of our lives is uncalled for, and we are tired of it. You can be on your way now," Andrew proclaimed as he released one final burst of energy that enveloped the house.

Moments later the house was quiet and empty, but completely destroyed. All of Bobby's furniture and belongings were charred and tattered, memories of his long life lay strewn all over the remains of the house.

"I guess it's time to move again," Bobby said with a sigh.

"Don't worry, we'll find another place," Andrew said, wrapping his arm around Bobby's shoulders. "Come on, let's get out of here."

The two walked through the remains of the house and out into the bright sunlight.

"So, sushi?" Andrew asked with a grin.

Bobby chuckled.

"Japan it is then," he said as the two men sprouted black wings and disappeared into the sky.

FRAN MAGLIONE

GROUND FLOOR

Trey Fields didn't often think about the people in his life. He never really had the time to. His recent promotion at work meant basically zero free time, a 60-hour work week, and a new ulcer to worry about. But, it also meant much more money to feed his already well-off bank account, so who was he to complain?

He had been gradually climbing the corporate ladder at an accounting firm for years, and as long as the checks continued to clear he would continue to climb. There was nothing Trey hated more than mediocrity, and there was nothing Trey loved more than being treated like royalty by a building full of people who had no idea what he was really like as a person.

Trey was probably a terrible person. Sure, he drank recklessly, he gambled, he played around with drugs, he did all the things that many other people also do, but there was so much more. There were things that he could go to prison for if he were found out (things he couldn't believe he'd gotten away with), and there was one event in particular that he vowed to take to the grave with him.

The day that Trey decided to pop into his boss's office for a chat was also the day he learned just how terrible he really was.

"Fields, come on in, my friend," his boss, Victor, called out. "Listen, there are some big changes coming soon, huge changes, and I want you in on the ground floor."

Victor walked over to Trey and put his hand on Trey's shoulder, squeezing lightly.

"I like you, Fields, I trust you," he continued, "so I have no problem telling you the news: we're finally merging with Morgan & Rochester."

Trey raised his eyebrows, mouth agape.

"Wow, sir, that is a pretty big deal," he said. "I have to say it's about damn time, too. Well done. What does that mean for us?"

"What it means, Fields, is a big fat raise for us," Victor said, "and also, probably trimming the fat from the rest of the place."

"You mean layoffs?" Trey asked.

"Massive layoffs, but whatever, they'll find other jobs, right? I'll need some help with this, though, Fields. There are way too many people for me to take care of at once," Victor said, leaning closer toward Trey and speaking softer. "As my right-hand man I need you to help me out. You can handle half of them, right?"

Trey paused for a moment, an unsettling feeling taking hold for just a second before he remembered what he was really there for.

"You got it," Trey said.

"Beautiful. Get started immediately, would you? I don't want to have to pay them for today," Victor said, clapping Trey on the back before walking away.

Trey steeled himself and stepped out of the office. Victor had wasted no time and was already weaving his way through cubicles, emotionlessly letting people go. Trey really admired him for that. Victor was completely disconnected from the world around him, and spared not a drop of sympathy for anyone who wasn't himself.

Adjusting his suit jacket and standing up taller, Trey walked over to the other side of the office and began emulating

Victor. He would quickly thank the employees for their service but regret to inform them that they were no longer needed at the organization. A generous severance package would be provided to them, which they could learn more about from HR. Then he would wish them well and move onto the next person.

The reactions varied: some were enraged, others sat in shock and had no reaction, a few cried.

"But, sir, please," one man pleaded, "my wife just had a baby. I need this job."

Trey had two children of his own but would still roll his eyes at people who spoke about their kids. Everyone always took parenting way too seriously, he thought. Children are remarkably self-reliant; they just need to be given the opportunity to take care of themselves.

"You will be provided with a generous severance package, which you can learn more about from HR. Best wishes to you," Trey said emotionlessly to the man before walking away.

By 10:00 a.m. the office was much emptier and very quiet, as the employees that were left seemed too frightened to make a peep. Victor and Trey met at the middle of the office when they were finished.

"Excellent job, Fields," Victor said. "Thank you for your help. Now, what do you say we go take an early lunch?"

Trey looked down at his watch and raised an eyebrow at Victor.

"A VERY early lunch, perhaps in liquid form," Victor added. "Let's go grab Johnson and Davis."

The two headed toward the exit, meeting up with their two cohorts on the way. Together the group walked into the hallway smiling and carefree like they hadn't just ruined the lives of nearly 100 people.

They piled into the elevator and chatted as it lowered to the ground floor.

"It's going to sound like a morgue in there the rest of the day, I'm sure," Johnson said with a laugh.

"Good, it never hurts to jerk the chain a little and strike

real fear into your workers," Victor said as he fished a cigar out of his suit pocket. "Sometimes they get a little too comfortable. They need to remember who they're here for."

He lightly patted his chest with the cigar a few times for emphasis.

*****

The four men sat at a booth in the local restaurant, the table littered with martini glasses and the remnants of several appetizers. They talked about the merger and what their new jobs would be like. But mostly they discussed what they'd be doing with their raises.

"I think I can finally take my wife on the trip she's been whining about for years. She wants to go to Jamaica. Maybe I can send her there without me," Davis said, laughing. "At least then it'll shut her up. Then I can spend a little time with Tammy. She saw a necklace at Tiffany's the other day that I just know she'd love. Maybe that'll be my first purchase."

"You're still messing around with that marketing girl?" Trey said. "How is it your wife hasn't found out yet? It's been like two years."

"Oh, look who's talking," Victor jumped in. "I think we all remember the conference in Salt Lake City, and then again in Minneapolis."

Trey suddenly began to sweat and laughed nervously.

"That's not the same, they were hookers," Trey stated plainly. "I'm not carrying on a relationship with any of them like Mr. Double Life over here."

The men laughed at the table and ordered more drinks.

Trey let the subject change quickly. None of them had to know anything more about what really happened during one of those conferences. No one could know about Jade, the tall brunette with piercing green eyes. She was expensive but worth it, if only she didn't give him so much trouble. He can still remember the sound of her giggle. But a memory flashing before his eyes of her lifeless body beneath him, eyes no longer bright but dull and unfocused, snapped him back to reality.

He asked Victor about his new Lamborghini. He was thinking of getting one for himself with his raise.

*****

It was close to 2:00 p.m. by the time the four executives made it back to the office, the smell of gin and vodka emanating from them. Being seasoned drinkers meant that they could hold their liquor well, but it was still obvious to everyone around them what they'd been doing for their elongated lunch break.

As Trey walked back to his office he could see the hatred in the eyes of the employees. They stared at him with disgust, and some of them muttered things under their breath. It didn't matter to him, though. He never gave any of them a second thought.

When he walked into his office Trey saw that he had a voicemail from his wife, Mary. She had heard about the layoffs, as one of them happened to be her nephew (thankfully Victor had handled that one for him), and she was livid.

Trey shrugged and deleted the message. He would deal with her later.

The afternoon continued as it usually did, full of conference calls and meetings, brainstorming sessions and chatting by the coffee machine. It was around 7:00 p.m. when Trey realized he should probably head home. He hesitated, though, as thoughts of his furious wife screaming at him kept him in his seat.

As if reading his thoughts, Victor appeared at the door of his office.

"It's only going to get worse the longer you put it off," he said to Trey. "Make sure the kids are in the room with you. Tether yourself to them if you have to. She won't go overboard if the kids are there."

With a final nod he left the office, and Trey started packing up his briefcase. He swiftly left his desk and turned out the lights. As he moved through the quiet and empty office he couldn't shake the terrible feeling he was experiencing. He figured he still had much more work to do if he ever wanted to reach Victor's level of apathy and nonchalance.

As he walked by one of the employees' cubicles he noticed a sign hanging up next to the man's computer. It read: "Abandon all hope, ye who enter here."

Trey chuckled and shook his head as he moved along. He reminded himself to ask the man to take it down tomorrow, though he did find it pretty funny.

Trey walked up to the elevator and pushed the down button. For a few moments nothing happened. He pushed the button again a couple of times and waited. Finally, he heard the sound of the elevator rising up to the fourth floor. With a ding the elevator doors opened and Trey sauntered inside and pushed the button for the ground floor.

He ran a hand through his hair and sighed deeply. It had been quite a day and it wasn't even over yet. He was bracing himself for the inevitable fight at home, but Victor's advice had been fairly decent. He would have to make sure he found the kids before his wife found him.

The elevator finally reached its destination as the letter G on the side panel lit up. Trey readied himself to get out but then realized that the elevator hadn't stopped. He examined the panel to see if he had pushed the wrong button, thinking maybe he had selected the basement instead.

He hadn't, and the elevator continued down below the basement anyway. There were no more levels to descend to in the building, yet the elevator continued to lower. Trey began to panic.

He frantically pushed every button he could find: stop, help, open doors, everything. Nothing had an effect on the elevator. It continued going down. Trey started banging on the doors.

"Hey! What's going on? Is anyone out there?" he yelled. "Someone help me! The elevator isn't working right!"

He heard nothing, and the elevator continued its descent. Trey started violently kicking at the doors now, still screaming out for help. The temperature in the elevator was gradually rising and Trey started to perspire.

After a while the elevator felt like it was slowing down. Trey braced himself against the handrail and stood perfectly still, barely breathing. The elevator stopped gently.

Trey swallowed hard as the doors opened and light poured in.

*****

Trey stepped forward out of the elevator and looked around him. The terrain was dry and wilted, the landscape decaying in front of him. In the distance he saw a castle and, as if being pulled by force, he began walking to it.

Suddenly two small figures appeared in the distance walking toward him; two young boys with curly hair like his wife's and tired eyes like his. They were his children.

"Tyler? Matthew?" he asked. "What are you doing here? Where are we? Am I dreaming?"

Figures walked silently around them, ignoring them. Everyone wore a similar blank expression.

"We're in limbo, dad," Tyler said. "You never baptized us, remember?"

"We've never even been in a church," Matthew added.

Trey furrowed his eyebrows, confused.

"What on earth are you talking about? What difference does any of that make?" he asked. "Now I know I'm definitely dreaming."

"It's not a dream, dad," Matthew said. "This is all real. You'll be visiting a lot of different places tonight; eight more, to be exact."

"The last place is where you'll be staying, though," Tyler said.

"What do you mean by staying?" Trey asked, as a fog gradually rolled in and began covering everything. He looked in the distance at the castle.

"What is that place?" he asked. "Why is it there?"

"It's a deception, dad," Tyler said. "Limbo is designed to look like heaven even though it's clearly not."

"Not even close," Matthew added.

"But you wouldn't know anything about deceiving people like that, would you, dad?" Tyler sneered.

"What's that supposed to mean?" Trey huffed.

The boys pursed their lips and glared at their father.

"It means you had better pay attention at the places you visit tonight and try to learn something," Matthew said. "It might be too late for your soul but you have to at least try to understand."

"Understand what?" Trey pleaded.

Trey suddenly realized that he had been unconsciously moving backward to the elevator again as his sons stood still, disappearing in the fog.

"Wait, don't leave. Stay with me!" Trey yelled out.

"Since when do you care if we're with you or not?" Matthew asked in a disgusted tone. "Just go, dad."

"Remember," added Tyler, "this is all because of you. All of it."

The boys vanished in the fog. Trey called their names out but received no response. Then the elevator dinged behind him. With one last look into the fog he turned and walked back into the elevator. The doors closed immediately and Trey felt the elevator begin another descent.

*****

When the elevator stopped and the doors opened, Trey hesitated. He still didn't quite understand what was going on or if he was dreaming. He looked out at the bleak landscape and felt a strong gust of wind. Bodies were blowing around in the breeze, flying all over the place. Trey stepped out of the elevator and was almost blown over by the breeze.

He looked around him trying to figure out where he was now and why he was there. Suddenly several women appeared before him. They were all familiar.

"You're frightened, Trey," one of the women purred, "how unlike you."

Trey recognized the graceful blonde with bright blue eyes

as a prostitute he had solicited years ago. She was his very first, actually, from a conference in Atlanta. No one knew about her, but he would never forget her.

"Sylvia," he said fondly with a smile. "How are you?"

"You don't care how I am," she sneered. "And are you really making small talk? Look where you are."

"Where are we?" he responded.

"You still don't get it, do you?" asked another woman, a young office assistant he had carried on an affair with at a previous job. He couldn't even remember her name. It was Mindy or Cindy or something. "You're in Hell."

"More specifically, you're experiencing the nine circles of Hell," Sylvia added. "Everything you've done in your miserable, wicked life has brought you here. We're here to remind you of your horrible life."

"I don't need a reminder," Trey said, frowning.

"Apparently you do," a third woman said. He recognized her as Breanna, the wife of a friend of his that he had slept with many times over the course of several years before he finally ended their relationship. "You just keep living your life as if you're not affecting anyone around you, but you are. We're all here because of you."

"I'm sorry to hear that," Trey replied, "but there's really nothing I can do about what's already happened."

"No, there isn't," Sylvia said angrily, "which is why you're here. It's why you'll remain down here once you reach the ninth circle."

"Remain down here?" Trey asked. "So, I'm dead?"

All three women rolled their eyes and sighed.

Then Trey remembered something (or someone, rather). He looked around but couldn't see her anywhere.

"She's not here, Trey," Sylvia said, reading his mind.

Trey sighed in relief.

"Well, that's good for her," he said.

"No, she just means that Jade's not in this circle," Breanna added. "You'll see her soon enough, though, don't you worry."

"You'll see a lot of familiar faces tonight," Sylvia said. "They will all be the faces of those you have wronged in your life, and of those you have dragged down into the mud with you. If you have any ounce of a soul left, take pity on them. They pity you."

Suddenly the wind picked up and Trey felt himself being lifted off the ground.

"Wait!" he called out. "Don't let them take me! Can't I just stay here?"

The women groaned.

"He doesn't even want to stay in the circle where his kids are? He's so terrible," Mindy or Cindy said.

"I hope Satan rips him a new one," Sylvia muttered.

As Trey was carried back to the elevator with the breeze he could still hear the three women laughing at him.

*****

As the elevator stopped its descent and the doors opened, Trey stood perfectly still.

"What if I don't want to go?" he said to the elevator. "You can't make me."

Just then the elevator started shaking violently before tipping forward, dumping Trey unceremoniously onto the ground outside like someone had just rolled some dice. He stood up and brushed his clothing off, glaring back at the elevator.

He turned around and looked out at the landscape. It was cold, raining, and the ground was wet with slush, which was now partially stuck to his clothing. As he walked on he heard talking and laughing in the distance.

"Trey, is that you?" a voice asked.

"Fields, my boy, come join us!" another voice yelled out.

Trey walked out of the icy mist and found Victor at a long table filled with men in suits that he recognized from a career full of corporate jobs: two former bosses, a few associates, and the two men that joined him and Victor at lunch just that day, Johnson and Davis. The table was littered with food and martinis. It looked as if a group of 50 people had been eating and drinking for days. One of the men was even snorting cocaine at the table.

"I heard you've been having a pretty eventful day," his former boss, Luke, yelled out. "Why don't you sit down and have a drink with us?"

"Sure!" exclaimed Trey as he looked around for an empty seat. "This circle seems way better than the others."

"It's really not that great," Davis said. "You can't get drunk, no matter how much you drink, the food has no taste, and it's so damn cold all the time."

"This slush gets on everything. I'm constantly cold and wet," Luke added. "But then again this is supposed to be an eternity of torture so I guess it makes sense."

"Oh, that's reminds me, he's not supposed to stay in this circle," Victor said. "I almost forgot. You've still got a ways to go before your final resting place, Fields."

"Sorry, no room at this table for you, friend," Johnson said.

"Guys, I really don't understand what's happening," Trey sighed. "I'm not dead. At least I don't think I'm dead, yet I'm wandering the circles of Hell in an elevator. And for some reason everyone I know is in Hell with me."

"Well, of course," Victor said. "What did you expect? Everything you do in your life impacts those around you."

"You brought this on yourself," Luke said.

"I just want to go home," Trey whimpered.

"Since when?" Victor laughed. "You hate it at home. Your kids drive you nuts and you can't stand your wife. You were trying to put off seeing her when I walked into your office tonight."

Victor picked up his martini glass and drank what was left. He held it in front of his face after and stared at it. Instantly the glass filled itself back up.

"And besides, you can't go home ever again, Trey," Victor said. "You're here for eternity. And so are we."

The ominous dinging sound of the elevator went off

behind him.

"You better go, Trey," Luke said. "You've got more to see."

"So is this goodbye?" Trey asked. "I'll never be able to see anyone in the other circles again?"

"Well, it doesn't really work that way," Victor said. "This isn't some office building, you know. But who knows? Maybe they'll make an exception for you."

Trey stood before the table, sad and defeated. He sighed heavily before turning around and walking slowly back to the elevator. The men resumed talking and laughing as the elevator doors closed in front of him.

*****

Trey didn't bother fighting it anymore, and when the elevator stopped once again he walked right out, ready to face what he needed to. But he still wasn't prepared for the sight before him.

There were dozens of people – hundreds, even. He recognized almost all of them. He knew they were employees, former coworkers, old friends, and even a few of his college roommates. They moved along in front of him, walking back and forth in lines grunting and panting. Each of them was pushing a massive heavy sack that appeared to be full of coins.

"They're pushing bags of money?" Trey asked.

He looked around at everyone. They were completely ignoring him, focused on their tasks.

"Hello? Anyone?" Trey said to the crowd. "Isn't someone supposed to talk to me during these stops? Like the ghost of Christmas past or something?"

The sounds of grunting and groaning filled the air. Not a single person acknowledged Trey's presence.

"Come on. How am I supposed to learn a valuable lesson here if everyone ignores me to push money around until they collapse?" he asked, growing more annoyed by the second.

He continued standing there staring at the crowd of people. There were elderly people, young men and women, and even a few children. Their groans grew louder; some of them even began sobbing and wailing, begging for mercy and for their freedom. He saw people he had barely even interacted with in his life, some former neighbors, friends both close and distant, a few of his business school professors, and every single person he and Victor had laid off that morning.

Everyone looked to be in tremendous pain and utterly exhausted. He looked at the faces of all of these people he knew and saw nothing but sadness and misery resulting from the bags of money.

"Oh…" Trey said softly.

He stood there for several moments longer, watching the scene in front of him with a sad, stoic expression. The elevator dinged and for a second he didn't move. He shed a single tear that rolled slowly down his face, and then he turned around and walked back to the elevator.

*****

The next time the elevator doors opened it felt even warmer than before. He looked out into the distance and saw a river. As he approached the river's murky, swampy waters he heard a gurgling sound. When he reached the bank of the river he saw a woman immersed up to her nose in the dark water. She was crying.

"Hello?" Trey asked. "Are you okay? Why are you crying?"

The woman stopped crying and stared daggers into Trey before bursting out of the water with a growl. He stepped back in shock, and then gasped when he realized who the woman was.

"Mary?" he breathed. "Oh, God, Mary. What happened to you?"

"You did!" Mary screamed. "You happened to me. You did this to me!"

She splashed through the water as she made her way to shore. When she reached Trey she roughly shoved him and he fell backwards.

"Mary, no!" he yelled from the ground. "Please stop. I didn't mean for this to happen."

"Oh, really?" she whimpered, voice cracking. "How do you figure? You chose your salary over your family. You chose greed and selfishness over a moral life. You chose your own desires over your friendships. You chose hookers over your own damn wife! A wife that once loved you very much."

Trey was now crying along with Mary.

"I'm so sorry, Mary," he whispered between sobs. He was still on the ground. "You have to believe me. I never wanted you to suffer. I never meant to hurt you."

"The way you choose to live your life affects me, Trey," she said solemnly. "It always has, and now it will for all eternity."

"Oh, Mary, no," Trey whined. "Come on, come with me. We can go back up to that first circle. We'll get our children and we'll be a family again. I'll do things right this time, I swear. We can get another chance."

"No, we can't," Mary whispered. "It's too late, Trey."

"It's not too late!" Trey yelled.

"Yes, it is!" Mary yelled back. "There's nothing that can be done now. And it's all because of you."

Trey swallowed hard and stared deeply into his wife's angry eyes.

"Mary, you have to know that I never meant to hurt you," Trey said softly. "You need to know that."

Mary sighed.

"Disregarding another person's feelings entirely means that you are trying to hurt them. That's how you hurt people, Trey. You only cared about yourself, and you never had anyone else's best interests in mind. You did mean to hurt me. You meant to hurt all of us. And you did hurt us."

Mary turned around and walked back into the river, the murky water swallowing her up immediately while Trey cried and called out her name, begging her to come back.

As he knelt by the river still sobbing, he heard the familiar ding of the elevator. He growled and leapt to his feet, spinning around to face the elevator.

"I am not ready yet!" he screamed. "I need more time!"

He turned back to the river and sat down, sighing deeply and looking into the water. He couldn't stop seeing the faces of everyone he had seen tonight, and he couldn't stop the hurt he felt from seeing Mary there, full of anger and hatred for him. It was so unlike her.

The elevator dinged again. Suddenly, the water began churning powerfully, splashing against his legs and trying to push him toward the elevator.

Trey sighed and dropped his head down as he stood up and walked slowly back to the elevator.

*****

As the elevator doors opened yet again, Trey walked out with his head still down, sullen and depressed. The horrors of his life's impact on everyone were finally catching up to him. The fact that he wasn't even done with this little journey yet made him even more depressed.

A flash of light in the distance caught his eye and he sighed and walked toward it. As he got closer he saw it was a tomb that was encased in flames. He saw two figures walk out of it and gasped in horror when he saw his elderly mother and father standing before him with pale, sunken faces.

"Not you, too," Trey said.

"Of course us, too," his mother said. "We made you. We're technically responsible for this mess."

"No, mom, you're not," Trey said. "Please don't think that. This is my fault, not yours. We're all here because of me."

"Sounds like he's finally getting it, at least," his father added.

"Do you remember when you were little and we would take you to church every Sunday morning?" Trey's mom asked.

"Of course I do," he chuckled. "You dragged me out of bed kicking and screaming most Sundays."

"We tried to instill some sort of spirituality in you," she continued, "some sort of moral decency. I guess we failed."

"No, mom, you didn't fail. Stop saying that," he pleaded. "I failed. In so many ways, I just failed."

"You lost your way so severely," his father said. "It's so hard to understand. You used to be such a good boy, helping out around the house, sharing your toys with your friends, even inviting the shy and quiet kids to all of your birthday parties. Now look at you. You don't blink an eye at ruining 100 lives so you can get a bigger paycheck, and we were lucky if we talked to you once or twice a year. We barely even got to see our own grandchildren."

"And now it's too late," Trey's mom said softly.

"I'm so sorry," Trey said as he began to cry again. "I didn't want any of this to happen. None of this was supposed to happen. You weren't supposed to suffer, I was. I'm the one who deserves eternity in Hell, not you!"

Trey dropped to his knees and slammed the ground with his fists.

"It's not fair!" he roared. "This has nothing to do with you!"

"It has everything to do with us," his mother said. "You've learned by now, haven't you? We are all affected by your actions and choices."

"You'd better start praying to whatever god or entity you believe in that the big guy downstairs is merciful with you," his father said. "Otherwise you're in for a long eternity."

His parents then turned and silently walked back into the tomb while Trey remained on the ground, crying and wailing until the elevator dinged once again.

*****

When the elevator doors opened this time, Trey found himself face to face with a tall, broad creature that looked like a man with the head of a bull. The creature silently gestured for Trey to follow, and Trey obediently walked behind him without a word.

As they walked along they approached a river of blood and fire. Bodies kept trying to lift themselves out only to be shot with arrows before falling back in. The screams and wails of the souls around him were deafening. There were some people even being chased around by vicious, snarling dogs. Trey continued to follow the creature.

They stopped walking when a woman appeared before them. She was tall with dark hair and was wearing a tattered black dress. Her green eyes were dull and lifeless. She appeared sickly and battered, covered in bruises and scars, and was holding a pile of blankets.

"Jade," Trey whispered.

The creature walked away, leaving Trey and Jade alone surrounded by screams and fire. Trey stepped closer to Jade and looked her over closely. The distinct bruising around her neck made his breath catch.

"You remember that, don't you?" she murmured.

Trey reached a hand out and gently touched the side of her face.

"I am so sorry I did this to you," he breathed.

"Sorry? You're sorry? You killed me, Trey!" she yelled.

Trey pulled his hand away from her face and grabbed onto his hair with both hands.

"I didn't mean to," he said as he closed his eyes. "I didn't want to! You made me! You wouldn't stop."

"You made me think that what we had was different, special," she sobbed. "We spent so much time together in those days. You were always so excited to see me again. You'd write me letters like you were a teenager in love. I saved every single one of them, did you know that? And I read them over and over. You said you were going to take me away from everything, and that you loved me. You said we were meant to be together."

"It was a nice idea, but you know that couldn't have really happened," Trey said. "It wouldn't have worked. It couldn't have."

"You didn't let it work!" she snarled back. "You didn't even try. You threw me out when you were done with me like I was a used tissue. And now, we're stuck down here forever."

"Jade, please," he whined, "don't be like this. You know how much I always cared about you."

He stared deep into her angry eyes and suddenly he was able to see the hotel room from years ago. He heard the banging on the door, and watched himself open it to find Jade standing there crying and asking why he was ignoring her calls, and that she had something important she needed to tell him.

He watched himself quickly pull her into the hotel room and slam the door ordering her to stop making a scene or else someone from work would hear. She continued crying as he shoved her around the room and slapped her, telling her to be quiet. He told her she shouldn't have come to see him, and that she was getting too attached to him. He suggested that maybe it would be better if they didn't see each other anymore.

Jade screamed that she loved him and that she needed him, and in a fit of rage Trey shoved her onto the bed yelling over and over that she needed to keep quiet. Finally, he watched himself crawl on top of her and wrap his hands around her delicate neck, squeezing as hard as he could while she writhed around beneath him.

He watched the life leave those beautiful green eyes as she collapsed in his hands.

Flashes of other memories popped into his mind. He saw himself putting her body into a garment bag that one of his suits was packed in, and then putting her on a luggage rack and wheeling her out to his rental car. He had dumped her body into a river that night. No one had ever found out.

Trey snapped back to reality and stared at Jade standing before him. He noticed she was now rocking the bundle of blankets back and forth in her arms, staring down at it lovingly.

"What...what is that?" he whispered, pointing to the blankets with a shaking hand.

Jade didn't respond, so he stepped closer and pulled a piece of the blanket away. When he looked down he saw a tiny, shriveled, purple creature that looked almost alien-like, squirming and making gurgling noises.

"It's your daughter, Trey," she said plainly. "She's your

unborn daughter that I was pregnant with the day you killed me. And now she's here, too."

Trey's jaw dropped and his eyes widened. He fell to the ground in a heap, sobbing uncontrollably. Jade turned and walked away from him just as the bull-headed creature arrived again. It took Trey by the arm and pulled him to his feet, and then pointed to the elevator as it dinged again.

*****

Trey sullenly walked out of the elevator and looked around him. He heard nothing and saw no one, just a single full-length mirror that stood in the middle of the empty landscape. Suddenly, he spotted the form of a winged creature with three heads flying high overhead. He stepped forward and approached the mirror.

He could barely recognize the reflection he saw. It was him, but he was pale, sunken and hunched over. He had dark circles and puffy bags under his eyes, and his eyeballs were bloodshot from crying. He saw the tear streaks going down his soot-covered face. He blinked and the reflection was gone, replaced with an image of him as a smiling little boy.

Trey sighed deeply and walked away from the mirror. He came to the edge of a cliff and looked down, spotting lots of people below. Some of them were tromping their way through manure while a demon with a sword was hacking off the body parts of others. People screamed and writhed in agony in a dark boiling lake, while others desperately tried to avoid a fire-breathing dragon.

Not wanting to see any more people being tortured, Trey turned around and walked back to the mirror. He looked at it one more time and saw that his reflection was slightly altered. The Mirror Trey's suit was clean and freshly pressed, his hair was neat, he looked healthy and tan, and he was smiling broadly. The word "Fraud" slowly materialized on the glass over his reflection.

With a huff, Trey turned around and was back at the elevator before it even dinged this time.

*****

As he angrily stomped back into the elevator he paused and tried to remember how many levels he had been on. He gasped when he realized he was at circle eight. The last circle he visited would be his last. Before he could run out of the elevator the doors quickly slammed shut in his face.

The elevator sprang to life again and began its final descent to the very bottom. Trey began to panic.

"No, no, no," he whimpered, shaking his head back and forth and pacing across the elevator. "I'm not ready. This can't be happening yet. I have to get out of here."

He looked around him, desperate for any possible solution when he looked up and noticed the ceiling panels. He started jumping up frantically, slapping one of the panels out of the way. Then he climbed up on the handrail and lifted himself up through the opening. Once he was on top of the elevator he replaced the tile and lay there silent and still.

Finally, the elevator stopped. After a moment the doors opened and a powerful blast of heat burst up through the elevator shaft. Trey held his breath.

He heard movement and shuffling around, some grumbling and growling, and what sounded like hooves clacking around on the elevator floor. Finally, the figure left the elevator and the doors closed. A second later, the elevator started going back up again.

Trey released a shuddering breath, and laughed to himself. He had done it. He had avoided an eternity in Hell — at least for now.

He lifted the tile back up and hopped down into the elevator. The temperature decreased as the elevator ascended and he was finally able to breathe normally again and stop sweating.

After several more minutes the air felt cleaner and fresher. Suddenly, he saw the light for the basement level of his office building light up on the side panel. He let out a whimpered shout and smiled, holding his face in his hands.

The elevator continued rising through the floors of the

building before stopping back on the fourth floor again. The doors opened and Trey practically hurled himself out onto the carpet of the office floor. Then, everything went black.

Moments later he felt a light tap on his shoulder. A quiet voice asked him if he was okay. Trey opened his eyes and saw the cleaning woman staring down at him concerned. He cleared his throat and stood up, brushing off his suit.

"Yes, I'm fine," he said, smiling at the woman. "I guess I've just been working a little too much. Thank you."

The woman smiled and nodded at him then walked down the hall. Trey just stood there staring around the office in amazement. He was back. He had somehow made it out. Maybe there was a reason he had made it out. Was he finally getting a second chance? He could apply all of the lessons he learned to his life. He would be a better husband to Mary, he'd take his sons to a baseball game, he would give the employees a raise. He would even call his parents. Everything would be better from now on. He was going to be a better person.

Trey smiled and turned around, staring at the elevator. Without hesitation he quickly turned to the left and headed for the door to the staircase, shaking his head and chuckling. It would be a long while until he could ride in an elevator again.

He flung open the door to the stairwell and started skipping down the stairs, whistling as he went. Finally, he reached the ground floor and muted, golden sunlight was pouring in through the cracks around the exit to the parking lot. He smiled again as he pushed open the door.

The blast of fiery heat caught him off guard and completely took his breath away. He tried to gasp for air as flames billowed out of the door and into the stairwell. A towering fur-covered demon with hooved feet and massive wings stood before him. Trey was unable to scream as the demon took hold of him and yanked him into the flames, slamming the door shut behind them.

FRAN MAGLIONE

ABOUT THE AUTHOR

Fran Maglione has been crafting creative short stories since the age of seven, which was also the year that she won her first national writing award. The accolades continued throughout her academic career and into her professional life as a local news reporter.

Thanks to an overactive and peculiar imagination, Fran has a habit of turning everything she experiences into a strange story in her mind. Putting it all down on paper just seemed like the logical next step. She has always had an interest in creepy stories and twist endings, but can neither confirm nor deny that this is a result of being born in Sleepy Hollow, NY.

Fran currently lives in southwestern Connecticut with her other half on a hill next to a river. Her hobbies include hiking, jogging, reading, taking photos, and predicting the ending of movies at around 20 minutes in.

Contact the Author
Twitter: @FranMaglione
Instagram: @Fran.Maglione
Facebook: @FranMaglioneAuthor

24462234R00076

Made in the USA
Middletown, DE
25 September 2015